Library
MacDonald Middle School
East Lansing, Michigan

Dawn at Lexington

Dawn at Lexington

by

NORMA WOOD JAMES

Illustrated by NEDDA WALKER

Library
MacDonald Middle School
East Lansing, Michigan

LONGMANS, GREEN AND CO.

NEW YORK · LONDON · TORONTO

Hannah Middle School Library
E. Lansing, Michigan

LONGMANS, GREEN AND CO., INC.
119 WEST 40TH STREET, NEW YORK 18

LONGMANS, GREEN AND CO., LTD.
6 & 7 CLIFFORD STREET, LONDON W 1

LONGMANS, GREEN AND CO.
20 CRANFIELD ROAD, TORONTO 16

DAWN AT LEXINGTON

COPYRIGHT · 1957

NORMA WOOD JAMES

ALL RIGHTS RESERVED, INCLUDING THE RIGHT TO REPRODUCE
THIS BOOK, OR ANY PORTION THEREOF, IN ANY FORM

PUBLISHED SIMULTANEOUSLY IN THE DOMINION OF CANADA BY
LONGMANS, GREEN AND CO., TORONTO

FIRST EDITION SEPTEMBER, 1957
REPRINTED MARCH, 1960

LIBRARY OF CONGRESS CATALOG CARD NUMBER 57–10526

Printed in the United States of America

Author's Note

AMERICAN HISTORY has provided this story. Jeremiah is only partly fictitious, since Henry Knox's journal states that his brother William and a servant accompanied him on the arduous trip to Fort Ticonderoga and back to the American troops half-circled about besieged Boston. That servant could have been a boy like Jeremiah Cutler.

Both sides suffered from the outrages of war. During the first year many British seem to have considered the rebellion as no more than a series of alarming antics. Allegiance to the Crown and to Home (England), they felt, would hold the colonies. It is true that many colonists felt a warm filial regard for the King—not as a person so much as a fatherly presence across the water. The Southern states particularly stressed that the quarrel was not with His Most Gracious Majesty, but with Parliament. New England pinned the blame on King George III where they thought it belonged, since many members of Parliament were outspokenly in favor of the Patriots' cause. ("American" in preference to "Whig" or "Patriot" seems first to have been used consistently after April 19, 1775.)

HM 70 - 868

In December 1775 Henry Knox, brother, and servant did camp overnight with prisoner of war John André because of crowded conditions at Fort George. Henry's letters reveal admiration for André and express delight at the lively discussions on various topics that went on all through the night. Neither young man could foresee, of course, their tragic next meeting almost five years later at Major André's trial. As to Benedict Arnold, his behavior was not beyond understanding. He felt he had lacked the cooperation of Congress, and he had suffered severe physical pain and mental anguish. Yet so had others, many more perhaps than history has been able to record. It seems, therefore, that it is not Arnold's treason which is unbelievable or amazing—it is the courageous vision of his contemporaries who held fast to the American dream.

N.W.J.

To
my son Dick

Chapter 1

JEREMIAH CUTLER added more split kindling to the fire. As its flickering warmth chased Boston's early dawn chill from the bookstore, he unwound his muffler, took off his coat, and began sorting the new shipment of books and stationery which had come from London a few days before. He worked quickly, hoping to have everything in order before the Knox brothers, Henry and William, arrived.

The new books he arranged on an eye-level shelf near the door, their gold-lettered spines prominently inviting inspection by the teachers, parsons, literary-minded ladies, and British officers too, who would soon enter the store. People flocked to Henry's establishment not only for good books but for good conversation. The London Bookstore had become one of the town's popular meeting places.

Jeremiah enjoyed his work, though it made him angry to be called "the bookseller's sweeper boy" by some of the British officers and Tory townspeople who gathered there. He was a bookseller's apprentice, and proud of it. In fact, he sometimes wished Henry would treat him like an apprentice rather than a younger brother to be watched over and protected. Henry seemed to forget that he would be

1

fifteen in the fall. Jeremiah was able to look out for himself —old enough to help more, too. That's why at dawn he had crept down the stairs from his garret room in the Knox house and hurried along the dark cobbled street to the store. He wanted to have the floor swept and the new stock sorted to surprise Henry and William.

Besides, today was a very special day. Patriots' Day was to be celebrated—Monday, March 6, 1775—since the fifth, the actual anniversary of the Boston Massacre five years ago, had fallen on Sunday. If the store opposite Savage's Court was in order they could close it in the afternoon and all go to the Old South Church a few doors away to hear Dr. Warren's memorial speech.

The books were arranged. The stationery was displayed on a narrow table near the fireplace. Jeremiah's dark-brown hair, tied at the nape of his neck with a narrow black ribbon, became disheveled as he hurriedly swept the hearth.

He was surprised and somewhat annoyed when the little bell over the door tinkled and Sam Ballard rushed in.

"Jeremiah!" Sam whispered hoarsely. "I must talk to you. It's important!"

"What now, Sam?" Jeremiah kept sweeping to let Sam know he was busy. "Can't be that some Britisher has thrown ashes on the coasting hill again. There has been no snow sledding for weeks."

"No, Jeremiah. Please listen," Sam begged, his straw-colored hair all askew.

Jeremiah put down his broom. Sam's freckled face was paler than any thirteen-year-old boy's should be. He beck-

"I must talk to you. It's important."

oned him toward the fire. "You are wrought up," he said. "What is it, Sam?"

"I was holding horses last evening for some British officers while they talked in front of the Tavern, and I heard them talking and laughing about Dr. Warren's speech today. It wasn't until later, after I got into bed, that I knew what they meant. They plan to arrest everybody at the meeting this afternoon for disorderly assembly."

"But it won't be!" Jeremiah protested. "It's our regular memorial of the Massacre."

"The British will make it disorderly. Lord Percy's ward, Roger, is to get a front seat and he'll have eggs in his pocket—"

"Of course!" Jeremiah cried. "And if Roger manages to throw one egg the meeting will get out of hand. There will be turmoil, maybe gunfire. The Boston Massacre started with a snowball fight and five of our men were killed before it ended."

"Even if there is no shooting, just disorder, the Redcoats will have an excuse to arrest Dr. Warren, Mr. Adams, and Mr. Hancock. Maybe your employer too. He's a lieutenant in the Boston Grenadiers," Sam said. "They'll probably imprison our militia captains also."

Jeremiah's heart beat furiously as he thought of Roger sneering at the militia men when they drilled, the Minutemen, people sometimes called them. He could well imagine Roger volunteering to disrupt the meeting. Roger, as his ward, expected a commission in the Northumberland Fusiliers of which Lord Percy was Major General. Then he would wear a scarlet coat faced with green and trimmed with gold.

Once Roger and Jeremiah had coasted, fished, and gone sailing together, but that was long ago, before the British King crippled Boston's sea trade and took away Massachusett's free charter because a group of angry townspeople refused to pay more taxes on the tea Britain shipped them and dumped it in the harbor. The Boston Tea Party, it was called now, and it had happened over a year ago, but because of it Boston was overrun with redcoated soldiers. Sometimes they even camped right on the Common. The Common had a smooth green lawn and walks shaded with elm trees. Boston people were proud of it. They wanted to keep it beautiful and they resented the redcoated trespassers.

Jeremiah turned to Sam. "I shall take care of Roger," he said, his lips thin with determination. "And, Sam, you had better tell Mr. Hancock or Mr. Adams. No need to worry Dr. Warren."

"I will, if I can find them," Sam agreed. "I'll be able to hear more of what the British are up to while I hold their horses."

"Yes," Jeremiah said thoughtfully. "I can listen to them right here in the bookstore."

Sam grinned. His eyes danced as he pulled his cap over his ears. "We are Sons of Liberty too, aren't we, Jeremiah?" he asked. "Aren't we?"

"We are, Sam. I for one can't wait to see Roger's face when he finds himself locked in Lord Percy's barn with his pockets full of smashed eggs." Jeremiah laughed. "I'll guard him myself until the meeting is over. Now please, Sam, get along. I have more work to do today than I planned."

After Sam left, Jeremiah finished sweeping. The morning sunshine began to stream in the back windows so he blew out the candles. Candles were scarce now.

Dropping cross-legged to the oval rug in front of the fire, he opened his Latin grammar to the page Henry had assigned for study. If he could save enough money, Jeremiah hoped some day to be learned enough to enter Harvard College in Cambridge, just a few miles outside of Boston. It had been his parents' fondest wish. Jeremiah's father had been lost at sea five years before, shortly after his mother had died of pneumonia. At that time Mrs. Knox, who had lost eight of her own sons, had taken ten-year-old Jeremiah into her home. Her loving care and the two Knox brothers' warm companionship had eventually healed his grief and loneliness.

But as time went on, Jeremiah realized that all the household expenses fell on Henry's shoulders. The Knoxes were not wealthy and, though they would deny it, he knew he added to their financial burdens. So one day he offered Henry the few pounds his parents had left him. Henry refused and advised Jeremiah to save the money for his education. Every so often Jeremiah would bring up the subject again, insisting he wanted to pay what he could toward his food and clothing. Each time Henry refused.

Then on the day Henry opened his bookstore Jeremiah, who had almost finished his elementary schooling, asked to work as an apprentice, and Henry had consented. "I understand your feelings, boy," he had said. "You want to be independent, and a bookstore is a fine place to continue your education."

Jeremiah knew how true this was. Henry had, during his own bookselling apprenticeship, acquired extensive knowledge in the classics and military science. He had also taught himself French and a little Latin.

It was finally agreed. William was to do the printing and binding and Jeremiah was to sweep, sort stock, and make himself generally useful around the new store.

How happy and proud Mrs. Knox had been that day in July when the London Bookstore opened, Jeremiah thought, as he poked the fire to a cheery glow. But the following December she had died.

"William is not strong," she had said to Henry just before she passed away. "Watch out for him, won't you, Henry? Take care of little Jeremiah too. I have come to love him as my own."

Kind-hearted Henry had solemnly promised his mother that he would take care of both boys. Henry had kept that promise, Jeremiah decided, as he tried hard to concentrate on his studying—earnest scholarship always pleased Henry —but the Latin verbs danced before his eyes in a perplexing way. His mind insisted on planning how he would stop Roger from reaching Old South Church.

In no time it seemed the door's overhead bell tinkled again. Henry entered, jovially calling, "Jeremiah, I am delighted to see you studying so seriously."

Jeremiah smiled up at his tall ruddy-faced foster brother, employer, and friend. He felt a little ashamed, for he hadn't been as studious as he appeared.

Henry ran his fingers lovingly over the new books on the shelf. "Very nicely arranged. Now, Jeremiah, you are a good lad, but it seems you are being a bit too good this morning. Could it be you hope to attend the meeting this afternoon to hear Dr. Warren?" he asked, cocking his head and smiling broadly. "Never fear, boy, you may go."

Just a few hours ago the meeting had been the reason for Jeremiah's eager work about the shop, but now he could not go. He must keep Roger and his eggs from causing a riot, a riot that would give the British an excuse to arrest Mr. Adams, Mr. Hancock, and Dr. Warren. Would he dare tell Henry the whole story?

Henry whistled cheerfully. He hung his long coat and tricorn hat on one of the wall pegs between the back windows. Jeremiah bent his head over his Latin grammar. "Henry," he said carefully, "I think I shall stay here in the shop this afternoon." He had decided not to tell about his plan, for Henry deplored what he called "the reckless use of force." "You and William, will be better able to enjoy the meeting if you know the shop is being tended, and Mrs. Knox will too."

Jeremiah knew that Lucy, Henry's wife of less than a year, would want to go to the meeting, though her father, an appointee of the British monarch, George III, highly disapproved of Dr. Warren and his Sons of Liberty meetings in the Green Dragon Tavern. Lucy's father was a Tory and her husband, Henry, was a Whig. Poor Lucy! The Tories in both the colonies and England upheld the King in all he did. The Whigs were for freely chosen government. There were many Whigs in England, Henry had told Jeremiah, who spoke out bravely against the King's unfair treatment of the American colonies.

Henry looked puzzled. He began winding a black-silk scarf about his mutilated left hand, as he always did when out in public. He had lost two fingers while hunting as a boy. This painful accident had made him realize how little he knew about firearms, and for years now he had spent his free hours studying military science, especially with regard to the new types of cannon. His knowledge of gunnery was valued by the Boston Grenadiers. Henry believed in "an orderly show of arms" to let George III know the colonists expected fair treatment.

"Well," Henry said finally, smiling once more, "if you would really rather stay here and study while we go to South Church, fine. We do have a sizable investment in this new stock. I couldn't afford to have it stolen or destroyed." He frowned. "As you know, the British Regulars need little excuse to enter and search any shop or private house."

The bell tinkled again and William Knox entered. He was as tall as Henry, but thinner and rather pale. His frequent cough caused his older brother much concern, though he rarely mentioned it because nineteen-year-old William did not like to be worried over. He often teased

HM76-868

Hannah Middle School Library
E. Lansing, Michigan

Henry about "acting like a mother hen" with respect to both himself and Jeremiah.

"No excuse at all," William said, as he lightly tapped Jeremiah on the head and went to the back of the store.

After hanging up his coat and hat, he uncovered a small printing press. The London Bookstore found it profitable to print seven-shilling pamphlets for people who were anxious to circulate their views on various subjects.

"They are a mean sort, some of those soldiers," William said as he bent over his boxes of type.

"Yes, they do act ill-tempered. That's because they don't want to be here," Henry answered. "Certainly we don't want them. But the King has so commanded."

Henry took a feather duster from the cupboard and began skimming lightly over the tables and chairs just as the door opened.

"Dr. Warren!" exclaimed Jeremiah, jumping to his feet. Mrs. Warren was a frequent visitor at the bookstore but her husband rarely had time for a visit. In fact, Jeremiah hadn't seen him in several weeks, not to talk to. He still treasured the day he had gone to the office on Hanover Street to have a boil on his elbow lanced. Dr. Warren's gentle hands had made it almost painless. Then they had talked man-to-man about Boston's dilemma. It had made him feel almost grown up.

Now the doctor's kind face turned toward Henry. "My wife wants a list of your new shipment." He smiled. "She is primping for this afternoon's meetings so I promised to stop by."

"I shall make out a list for Mrs. Warren," Jeremiah said eagerly.

As he wrote, Dr. Warren and Henry discussed the sorry plight of Boston, as everyone did these days.

"Our fishing fleets haven't been allowed to put to sea for almost a year," Dr. Warren commented, after Henry spoke of the scarcity of whale oil for the street lamps. "If it weren't for the other colonies sending us food, Henry, we would have more hunger too. Is it any wonder every movement of His Majesty's army is known ahead of time here in Boston? So many are idle with nothing to do but watch."

"And as they watch they become more rebellious, and rightly so!" Henry said with a forceful nod. "The London publishers warn me that each shipment may be the last. Any day the King is apt to dip his fingers into the bookselling business too."

Dr. Warren put the list Jeremiah handed him carefully in his vest pocket. "Until this afternoon, gentlemen," he said with a little bow. "I shall have four seats reserved."

"That's thoughtful of you, Doctor," said Henry, "but just three will be needed. Jeremiah isn't going."

Dr. Warren's kind gray eyes turned to Jeremiah. He looked a little taken aback.

"How I wish I could tell him why I am not going," thought Jeremiah. "Now he must think I don't want to hear his speech and I do, I do!"

The doctor nodded good-by and left the store. Henry

went on with his dusting and William remained silent as he concentrated on setting type.

"Taxes, taxes," Henry mumbled. "The Molasses Act, the Sugar Act, the Stamp Act, and now the Port of Boston closed. The King himself, by his unjust measures, has united the colonies as never before."

"Mr. Revere says the courier riders have united the colonies too," said Jeremiah, hoping Henry would continue talking and forget to treat him like a child who could not be expected to understand.

"The couriers!" Henry laughed. "Since Mr. Revere is one himself he would naturally think them important. They are," he added soberly. "Within two weeks a new outrage by the King's men here in Boston is known to the Carolinas and Georgia. One of our couriers, Mr. Brown, has just returned from Fort Ticonderoga on Lake Champlain."

"News from there can't help Boston. It's so far away," Jeremiah protested.

"Ah, Jeremiah, it is far away, near Canada, but the British have at the fort great supplies of cannon balls, powder, all kinds of artillery." His eyes grew brilliant. Lucy often said her young husband loved books and firearms better than eating, and Henry had an enormous appetite. "With such weapons," he went on, "Fort Ticonderoga would be very important to either side should war come."

Jeremiah marched to the center of the oval rug and stood very straight. He hoisted an imaginary gun to his shoulder. "On the day I am sixteen," he said, "I shall join the militia and have my own musket, powder horn, and bullet mold."

Henry looked alarmed but William chuckled.

"It is my duty according to the Massachusetts Provincial Law," Jeremiah said. "Why must it be only men from sixteen to sixty? I shall have to wait a year and a half."

"Wait you shall, boy. It is the law," Henry said sternly. "There is too little regard for law and order here now. It is understandable with things as they are, but if war should come we must become organized, orderly, and find a leader able to command the respect of all."

"Mr. Hancock or Mr. Adams?" Jeremiah asked, glad that Henry was in a talkative mood.

"No, not Mr. Hancock," Henry said. "A fine man, but too given to displaying his wealth to win the devotion of our poor, ragged militia men. Not Mr. Samuel Adams either, nor his lawyer cousin John. Sam and John admit they lack military knowledge. No, I am thinking of Colonel George Washington and so are others. It was Colonel Washington's courageous speech six years ago that united the colonies in a boycott of British merchandise. Sam Adams was mightily impressed by Colonel Washington at the Continental Congress last fall. The Colonel upheld Dr. Warren's Suffolk Resolves to the letter. Let us pray the second Continental Congress meets again in Philadelphia and settles the matter of leadership. We need a commander in chief soon, before it is too late."

"Mr. Revere has told me of Colonel Washington's bravery during the French and Indian War but, Henry,

Mr. Washington is a Virginian. Do you mean all the colonies will be in this fight to free Boston when it comes?"

"Jeremiah, I did not say it must come. Very likely our differences with the Crown will be settled peacefully," Henry said rather sharply. Jeremiah knew he had suddenly remembered the ten years difference in their ages.

"Jeremiah, I warn you, should you become involved with Paul Revere and the Sons of Liberty you are apt to be imprisoned for treason. Those charged with treason, as you well know, are taken to England for trial and very often hanged."

William spoke out boldly from the back of the store. "You yourself, Henry, have just been talking treason. And I have seen you talking very often of late with the landlord of the Green Dragon Tavern. Everyone knows the Sons of Liberty hold their meetings there and that the landlord gathers information for them."

His brother's full face grew red. "I was wrong to speak to you boys of such serious matters. Should my words cause either of you to act rashly I would never forgive myself. I promised Mother to care for both of you until you come of age. With God's help I shall do it. You, Jeremiah, are still a boy, not yet fifteen. Take care! Boys often think too highly of their own knowledge." Henry held up his scarf-wrapped left hand and said gravely. "I did."

Jeremiah wisely said no more. "How glad I am," he thought, "that I didn't tell about Roger and the eggs and what I plan to do." In spite of Henry's warnings he still intended to do all he could to keep Dr. Warren's meeting from becoming a riot.

Chapter 2

AFTER DINNER—the best that Lucy could manage with food so scarce—Jeremiah went back to the store on Cornhill, leaving Henry and William free to escort her to the meeting. The afternoon flurry of customers did not usually begin until three o'clock. Jeremiah had the store to himself.

The minutes ticked by and soon people began walking or riding past the bookstore on their way to the Old South Church.

A small detachment of redcoated soldiers gathered in front of a tavern diagonally across the road. They laughed raucously. One stood leaning against a hitching post, polishing his sharp bayonet in a menacing way. Every now and then two or three would walk to the corner and look down School Street as though they expected someone.

Jeremiah knew he must leave the bookstore neither too late nor too soon. He wished now that he and Sam had made a careful plan. Next time they would. Despite Henry's words of caution, he knew there would be a next time and a next. If he couldn't join the militia, he would help the Sons of Liberty until Boston received fair treatment from the King.

It was time to leave, he decided. He carefully locked the door behind him.

Stuffing his muffler into his coat pocket, he stepped out into the street to find Sam and his sister, Lydia, walking toward him. Jeremiah, fearful of arousing suspicion, briskly nodded his head and said very low, "Keep walking, there's a soldier watching us." For the man had replaced his now gleaming bayonet at the end of his musket and stood staring at them.

Lydia, who was sixteen, giggled and turned her merry smile on Jeremiah. "Don't blush, Jeremiah, I am only pretending to flirt with you. Listen! Roger will leave Lord Percy's house in about five minutes."

"How do you know?"

"Sam and I went to Lord Percy's house and told his servant we wished Roger to accompany us to the meeting." Lydia's curls bounced beneath her brown-velvet bonnet as she tossed her head in a flirtatious way for the watching soldier's benefit.

"Roger came to greet us in the hall," she continued. "He looked so pleased that we had asked him, Jeremiah. I must admit I disliked the deception." Lydia sighed and clasped her small gloved hands together. "But he in turn deceived us, for he said he felt a little ill and did not plan to leave the house. Yet he was dressed to go out in cream-colored breeches, brocade vest and dark-blue coat. He wore a freshly laundered linen neckcloth too, and new boots."

"Lydia," bawled Sam in his best young-brother fashion,

"I am tired of forever waiting while you talk to your beaux."

The reason for his outburst was soon apparent. The watching Redcoat had started across the road toward them. Jeremiah's heart pounded but Lydia, though her eyes grew round, turned quickly and flashed a smile at the approaching Britisher. Slowly she began to walk away from the bookstore, chattering pleasantly. Before he knew it, the soldier found himself a hundred yards down the street. A shout of derisive laughter from his fellows in front of the tavern brought him scampering back, but by this time Jeremiah was on his way toward Lord Percy's house.

As he walked toward Winter Street with a casual air, he hoped his plan to entice his victim to the barn would be successful. Roger had often frankly admitted to Jeremiah that, next to becoming a Fusilier, he wanted most to add to his impressive collection of descriptive essays on the animal and bird life of New England. George III and Queen Charlotte would deem it a service to the Crown. They might even someday think him worthy of knighthood. To be Sir Roger Hart!

Jeremiah pondered. He could imitate an owl better than a blue jay. The owl it would be.

Fortunately there were no servants about when Jeremiah approached the house from the rear. The high black coach with its gilded wheels was nowhere in the barn. Neither were the six coal-black horses that pulled it. Lord Percy was evidently out on a special call, or perhaps he was with General Gage awaiting news of the patriots' arrest. Jeremiah considered his absence a stroke of luck.

Where he stood behind a clump of bushes in the side yard, he had a good view of the front door through which Roger soon should emerge. He practiced his owl call softly. Yes, it was good. It sounded very real. It should make Roger curious enough to follow its sound, eventually into the barn.

Jeremiah started as the front door opened and Roger stood on the little entrance porch. He looked very elegant. His freshly powdered hair showed his high forehead and long thin nose to advantage, as did the black hat he adjusted carefully.

Roger was slender, but as the March wind blew open his coat Jeremiah saw that his breeches bulged suspiciously about the pockets. It was true then about the eggs!

A moment's panic overcame Jeremiah; his throat was dry and tight. Then softly from his lips, but clearly perfect, came the owl's call.

Roger turned his head and listened. Again the hoot, a little louder, and he went down the steps, disappearing for a moment behind a big oak tree. Jeremiah's hopes crashed. Roger was not being taken in by the ruse. But wait! He was tiptoeing toward the bushes where Jeremiah hid.

Hooting once more, Jeremiah stealthily backed from one concealing bush to another toward the open barn door. Roger moved closer, walking a bit clumsily in his new boots. It should be easy to throw him off balance, Jeremiah thought.

Roger leaned against the hay bales as though his feet

hurt. In a flash Jeremiah darted behind him. With lightning speed he pinned his arms behind his back and tied them securely with his muffler.

"You must be mad, Jeremiah!" Roger said haughtily when he saw his captor's face.

"Am I?" asked Jeremiah grimly. He clapped his hands hard against Roger's bulging pockets, smashing the eggs. They crackled as they broke, and the yolks seeped through the cream-colored broadcloth.

Roger glared. Angry red spots appeared on his thin face but before he could shout, Jeremiah bound his gaping mouth with a big clean handkerchief.

Now that the feat was accomplished, Jeremiah grew uneasy. As the minutes dragged by, he realized the seriousness of his act. He had bound and gagged Lord Percy's ward and Lord Percy was His Majesty's representative in Boston. This was the rash act Henry had feared, and both he and William could be accused as conspirators in their young friend's plot.

As time passed, Roger's anger faded. A pleading look appeared in his eyes and Jeremiah, certain that the meeting must now be over, and that he and the Knox brothers were headed for prison anyway, took pity on his captive.

Loosening the kerchief, he said, "I am sorry, Roger, but I had to do something. You were planning to start a riot at the meeting with those eggs, weren't you?"

"I was. Once the Sons of Liberty are disbanded, there will be loyalty to the King and peace here in Boston."

"There is loyalty here," Jeremiah said firmly. "Loyalty

to the charter, our free government, which the King has taken away."

"We have argued before. We cannot agree." Roger brushed back his hair. He picked up his hat and stood up straight with difficulty. "Jeremiah," he said, gingerly pulling at his sticky, egg-stained breeches, "would you mind not telling anyone about this?"

It was Jeremiah's turn to gape. "You're not going to tell Lord Percy?"

"Certainly not! My guardian knew nothing about this. Neither did General Gage, though I believe they would have been grateful had we succeeded. But Lord Percy did expect me to report on the meeting. I shall have to tell him I fell—which I did, into your trap—and hurt my foot, which is true. These new boots pinch dreadfully." Roger grinned wryly as he said, half to himself, "Now I know what Lord Percy meant when he said not even a Caesar could rule Boston."

Jeremiah put out his hand. "Roger, word of honor, I shall tell no one." Pride, he thought, was saving them all from arrest.

Roger ignored his former friend's outstretched hand. Having straightened his collar and vest he drew himself up haughtily. "Next week I shall become an ensign in the Fusiliers. It would be most embarrassing should this—this little happening get about. A Northumberland Fusilier held captive by the bookseller's sweeper boy. Indeed!"

Jeremiah clenched his fists, then jammed them into his pockets. He must control his temper. The safety of everyone depended on it. The escape had been narrow enough as it was. "Indeed, indeed!" he angrily mocked.

"Selling books is an honorable trade and sweeping is honest labor." The tone was condescending. "So is blacksmithing, fishing, weaving, and grinding grain into flour. But tradesmen are not soldiers, and these militia bands are nothing but tradesmen. Their marching is terrible, their uniforms a patchwork mixture. Some drill on the Common in ragged homespun."

"We would not be so dressed had not the King chosen to punish Boston so cruelly."

"Once Boston pays for that Tea Party in the Harbor—The sum is high, I agree, but—"

"Were it only one shilling," Jeremiah shouted defiantly, "Boston would not pay!"

Roger shrugged his shoulders as though he were no longer interested. He was thinking, Jeremiah knew, of the scarlet coat he would wear next week, of the gold braid, the high stiff stock under his chin, and the wide cartridge belt strapped diagonally across his chest from his left shoulder to his right hip. Roger would have a musket for his very own, Jeremiah thought enviously.

"As I said before," Roger remarked coldly, walking toward the back of Lord Percy's house, "our arguments reach nowhere. You are blind to what is best for Boston and for all the colonies, for that matter. Cut off from the King's protection, these settlements would soon become wilderness again. Jeremiah, you won't tell about this afternoon?"

"I gave you my word before," Jeremiah answered curtly.

As he climbed the fence behind Lord Percy's barn and headed for the bookstore, he heard the back door slam.

Later that evening after supper Lucy looked up from her sewing. "Henry, dear, did you tell Jeremiah what an excellent lecture he missed this afternoon?"

"Yes, my love, and I told him how the British soldiers trooped into the church at the last minute. Dr. Warren had to climb in the side window to reach the pulpit."

"Was there any disturbance?" Jeremiah asked cautiously.

"Not a bit," Henry answered.

"But," said William, "it was strange. Did you see how the soldiers kept glancing toward the door expectantly? It was as though they awaited someone."

"Yes, William," agreed Lucy, rocking comfortably, "I noticed that too. They trooped out after Dr. Warren's speech, looking very disappointed."

Jeremiah turned his head to hide his smile.

Chapter 3

WHEN JEREMIAH gave his word to Roger he was sure he could keep it. Because Sam had been unable to find either Mr. Hancock or Mr. Adams before the March 6 meeting, no one knew about the plan to stop Roger and its successful outcome except Sam, Jeremiah, and Roger himself. All three wanted it kept secret. Roger feared embarrassment. Jeremiah and Sam feared the wrath of Lord Percy and the British Governor General Gage, which could involve their loved ones. The secret would be well kept, Jeremiah thought.

He had forgotten about Lydia, Sam's sister!

Soon the "egg story" was whispered from one eager rebel listener to another. What a good joke on the King's overbearing Redcoats! Lydia had evidently shown some caution, for no names were mentioned. "One of our boys who helps tend shop," was the way the young hero was described.

The story reached Henry again and again, but only, of course, when the bookstore on Cornhill was free of British officers and Tory townspeople who sympathized with the King.

As the weeks went by, Jeremiah knew that Henry was going over in his agile mind all the boys who hadn't appeared at the meeting. There were only a few who "helped tend shop."

Henry never voiced his suspicions, but Jeremiah would look up to find he was being watched.

At sundown on Saturday, April 8, after William had left, Jeremiah banked the fire in the bookstore while Henry went around locking cupboards and windows in preparation for the Sabbath.

"I have some good news for you, Jeremiah," Henry said. "Professor Parkson of Concord, who retired from teaching just a few years ago, has consented to board and tutor you for two months. Isn't that splendid? You do need help with your Latin."

"Oh, no!" groaned Jeremiah. Another rash act was feared. Henry was doing what he thought best. He took very seriously the promise he had made his mother. But why must Jeremiah leave Boston now?

There was a tense quietness in town. The Redcoats were being unusually polite and orderly, as though they had been told to lull the people into a false sense of security. The increased fortifications by the British across the Boston Neck belied their peaceful manner.

Boston jutted into the harbor. With shipping forbidden and the Neck barricaded too, the town would be completely cut off. Jeremiah knew that all winter the rebels had been squirreling away their powder, ball and guns in surrounding settlements. Farmers could usually pass by the guards at the Neck unmolested. Under their hay loads were concealed the rebels' weapons of war. But now that the British seemed intent on trapping Boston by closing the Neck, the Sons of Liberty had urged the people to hurry the transporting of all firearms out of Boston.

Jeremiah remembered the friendly wink Dr. Warren had given him just the other day, as though he too knew who the boy of the "egg story" was. Dr. Warren was President of the Committee of Safety, and he told Jeremiah to report any unusual movement by the British soldiers.

"Boys can run about more easily than men without arousing suspicion," he had explained. "Not that I would entrust this work to every boy, Jeremiah." It had been agreed that Sam Ballard could help, too.

All information was to go to Dr. Warren, Paul Revere, or the landlord of the Green Dragon Tavern where the Sons of Liberty met. Mr. Adams and Mr. Hancock were keeping out of sight by visiting at different homes, because it was rumored the King had ordered their arrest for treason.

Something important was bound to happen soon in Boston, Jeremiah thought dejectedly. Now, because of Henry's dutiful concern for his welfare, he wouldn't be here. Only Sam would be able to help Dr. Warren.

"Henry," he pleaded, though he knew it would do no good, "I don't want to go to Concord. I can't—"

"We both know why you don't want to go, and why I want you to go," Henry said gently. "I believe in this rebellion too, but it must be in the hands of mature men, not half-grown boys. Jeremiah, until you grow up—"

"Grow up! I'm taller than most men now!"

"You know very well what I mean," Henry answered, his usually jolly face growing serious as he pulled open the door and went out into the street. He waited for Jeremiah to follow. "We shall say no more about it. On Monday morning at six o'clock be ready to mount the horse I have hired. William will accompany you as far as Lexington. You'll find Concord to your liking, I am sure. Professor Parkson's wife and your mother were friends. You will feel at home there."

"Very well, Henry," Jeremiah said with a resigned sigh. "I shall go to Concord, but I shall pay my own expenses, including the horse's hire."

"As you wish," said Henry gravely.

Jeremiah touched Henry's sleeve. "I'm sorry you're disappointed in me," he said.

"Disappointed?" Henry exclaimed. He looked surprised, then fondly thumped him on the back. "Don't think that, boy. I am proud of your patriotic feelings. I understand, truly I do. But I don't want any harm to come to you."

Jeremiah felt relieved, though a little chagrined as always at Henry's overprotectiveness.

On Monday morning Lucy knocked at Jeremiah's bedroom door at five o'clock.

"Here, boy, some hot water for washing," she said, as she set the steaming kettle on the rag rug in front of his washstand and placed a lighted candle in a tall brass holder next to it.

Lucy's paper hair curlers were covered with a lace-flounced cap. Her round young cheeks were rosy, as though she herself had bathed in ice water.

"I shall miss you, Jeremiah. Mind now, we're only sending you off because we think it best, and only until things quiet down here in Boston. Oh, dear, I hope they do," she added earnestly. "Here's a little gift for you," she placed two slender volumes on the washstand: *Sermons for Young Men* and *Robinson Crusoe*.

After Jeremiah thanked her, she blinked and bit her lip, then swiftly left the room, her long blue wrapper trailing behind her. Poor Lucy, if war came her husband would be fighting against her father and brother. There would be many in her predicament, he suddenly realized.

When William and Jeremiah trotted into Lexington, some farmers were already guiding their plows behind yoked oxen. The boys reined in their horses near the triangular village green.

William's saddle creaked as he leaned over and clapped the boy's shoulder affectionately. "A surprise for you, Jeremiah! That horse is not hired. She's yours! Henry bought her for you."

Before he could stutter his thanks, William wheeled his own horse around and, with a cheery wave of his hand, headed back toward Boston.

After checking the straps on the small leather trunk behind him, Jeremiah heeled his horse into a canter. The sharp morning breeze stung his cheeks. The air had the sweet moist smell of green shoots newly sprung from the thawed brown earth. As the sun warmed his back, he forgot his unwillingness to leave Boston. It was good to be in the country on a clear April day.

The horse Henry had so generously given him proved lively. The road unwound easily beneath her hoofbeats. A fine smooth-gaited mare. He would call her Rebel, even though William had said her name was Nellie. Some patriots didn't like being called rebels. Mr. Revere, for instance, considered it an insult. But Jeremiah liked the sound of it. Rebel his horse would be.

The road curved. A high ridge loomed at his right. Rebel swiftly cantered around the curve, and there at the end of the ridge lay Concord—the spired church where the Reverend Emerson preached, the two taverns where the King's misdeeds were thoroughly discussed each evening, the courthouse, and a cluster of twenty or more private houses looking frosty white in the morning sunshine. One belonged to Professor Parkson, and to Jeremiah it would be home for two months. He slowed Rebel to a walk as he entered the village.

The Parkson house, Henry had told him, was directly across the road from the bridge. Jeremiah found it easily. It was small, square, and white, with a low porch across the front and a wide window on either side of the door.

The door opened before he finished looping Rebel's reins through the ring of the iron hitching post in front of the picket fence. A hoarse voice called, "Come in, come in."

Jeremiah swept off his broad-brimmed hat and walked up

the stone-slab path carrying the small trunk under his arm.

Professor Parkson, tall, incredibly thin, silver-haired, clasped the boy's outstretched hand.

"Welcome, Jeremiah," he said, peering over his pinch-nose glasses. "You favor your mother, do you? She was brown-haired too. Ah, yes, the smile is the same, lopsided and a little shy. No need to be shy with us, boy. Come right in. Mrs. Parkson is anxious to meet you."

Mrs. Parkson was perched on the edge of a chair by the fire. When she rose and walked toward him, Jeremiah saw she was as tall and gaunt as her husband, and as warm in her welcome.

"It has been so long since we had a boy in the house, Jeremiah," she said. "Your room is at the head of the stairs. It's an attic room, but comfortable, and from your window you can see the river. I hope you will enjoy your stay with us. Take your trunk up. Then we shall all have a bite to eat."

"After which we shall tackle Cicero." The old Professor smiled. "The tales of the Roman Empire are most interesting when read in the original Latin."

"Thank you, ma'am, sir," Jeremiah said politely. "It is most kind of you to have me."

The attic room was comfortable, as Mrs. Parkson had promised. It had a big bed, piled high with feather comforters, and in a china bowl on the washstand stood a fat blue-and-white pitcher filled with warm water. From his window he could see the river, the bridge, and the hills beyond. There, according to Sam, the rebel arms were stored in Colonel Barrett's barn. Sam had been frankly envious of Jeremiah's trip to Concord.

"If there's trouble," he had said, "it will start there and you'll be right in the middle of it." The British, he had implied, planned to attack not Boston, but Concord. That sounded like a doubtful rumor, thought Jeremiah, as he looked out the window. No town ever looked more innocently peaceful, and dull.

His room, the whole house, smelled like dried flower petals, musty and old, like Cicero's Latin. Then he was ashamed of himself, for the Professor and his wife were so kind and so happy to have him.

To keep from thinking, he busily washed his face, brushed his hair, and wiped the dust from his buckled shoes. Still he couldn't help the wave of homesickness that overcame him. He missed Henry's booming laughter, William's good-natured teasing, and Lucy's rosy cheeks. He missed the bookstore and the bustle of Boston.

His stay in Concord, he decided as he went downstairs, would be endlessly dreary.

Chapter 4

"To arms! To arms! *The British are coming!*"

Jeremiah buried his head under the bedcovers, wishing his nightmares would not seem so real. He had been translating Cicero and conjugating Latin verbs for over a week now, and his sleep each night had been restless, filled with disturbing dreams.

"To arms! To arms!" Again came the shout, followed by a roll of drums and the clanging of bells.

Jeremiah sat bolt upright in bed. This was no dream!

He ran to the window, pulling on his breeches and tucking his nightshirt inside. Two men were running over the bridge toward the house, holding aloft flaming pine knots and shouting, "To arms! The British Regulars are coming!"

There was a clatter of hoofs, another roll of drums, a swelling hum of angry voices. All the while the bells pealed, louder and louder.

When Jeremiah ran down, Mrs. Parkson was standing alone at the foot of the stairs. She turned to him calmly and said, "Dr. Prescott brought the news. The British are leaving Boston by water."

"Not by land, across the Neck they have fortified?" Jeremiah asked, surprised.

"No. It was quite clever of them, but not clever enough. They were carefully watched, and Mr. Revere had a signal arranged with one of his friends. This friend, Captain Pulling, was to hang one lantern in the steeple of North Christ Church if the British left by way of the Neck, and two if they left by water. Two lanterns were hung in the steeple, so our couriers knew immediately that the British were embarking in boats on Back Bay."

"Is it the store of arms here in Concord they are after?" Sam had been right after all.

"Yes. They plan to arrest Mr. Hancock and Mr. Adams at the Clark parsonage in Lexington, capture their records of all 'treasonable' meetings, and then march here to Concord to confiscate our store of arms, kill three birds with one stone, you might say."

"Have Mr. Hancock and Mr. Adams been warned?"

"Oh my, yes," the old lady answered with satisfaction. "Paul Revere did that first thing, and all of our express riders are spreading the news about the planned attack on Concord. Right now Minutemen from all over are on their way here."

"Where are the British now, ma'am?"

"Let me see, it is almost two o'clock in the morning." She pursed her lips, then laughed. "They must be wading through marshes and across streams by now. They are not going to use the bridges, you see. They fear we shall hear them tramping across the planks." She laughed again.

"Why, Dr. Warren's Committee of Safety knew General Gage's plans before his own soldiers did."

Jeremiah laughed, too.

"You are to meet the Professor at Wright's Tavern on the square, Jeremiah," Mrs. Parkson went on. "He's with Captain Minot's company, all old men and boys, but spirited!"

He ran all the way to the square, shrugging into the sleeves of his coat as he went.

"I suggest," an old man was shouting from atop a table when Jeremiah entered the tavern, "that we send another messenger to Lexington. Reuben, the saddler, has been overlong in returning."

There was a mingled shout of agreement, a medley of old and young voices.

"A good rider," the old man continued, "that's what we need, and a good horse."

"Sir! Sir!" Jeremiah came forward waving his hand. "I have Rebel—that's my horse's name, sir—a good swift mare, and I know the way to Lexington."

"Let him go!" a voice shouted.

Professor Parkson said in a low voice: "You are tall, boy, but I know you are not yet fifteen. I am not sure I should let you go. This could be a dangerous errand. Our three regular express riders have been arrested by the British, Dr. Prescott tells us."

"Please, Professor! I shall take care. Dr. Warren appointed me his messenger in Boston," he pleaded.

"Did he? Well, he is a wise young man. If he trusted

your caution, we can," said the Professor. "Being a rebel messenger is more to your liking than studying Cicero, is it?" he asked, a twinkle in his eye. "I do not blame you, boy. Why read history when we are living it? Saddle Rebel, and be off. God go with you."

It was less than six miles from Concord to Lexington, but because it was dark and because he had been warned not to use the road and to walk his horse, Jeremiah did not arrive at his destination until after four o'clock in the morning.

He guided Rebel cautiously out of the woods and approached Lexington's triangular village green where he and William Knox had parted just nine days ago. It was very quiet, and dark except for a light in the nearby tavern.

All at once strong hands snatched Rebel's reins, and a low voice growled, "Who goes there?"

As he was led, still astride Rebel, toward the lighted tavern, Jeremiah told his name and presented the slip of paper Professor Parkson had given him.

The low voice became friendly. "No news of the British yet, boy. We have a scout a mile down the road. Best come into the tavern. Rest yourself a while before you return."

Jeremiah dismounted. The strong hands gripped him by the shoulders. "Your name is Jeremiah Cutler, why, you must be the bookseller's apprentice. The one who—the eggs—ho! ho!" The big man threw back his head and roared with laughter. "Look!" he said as they entered the tavern where men were standing or sitting in groups of three of four. "Look, I have here the young patriot who smashed the eggs."

The owner of the strong hands was John Parker, Captain of Lexington's Minutemen.

Jeremiah had just begun to tell Captain Parker that the men of Concord were hiding the store of powder and ball in deep furrows near Punkatasset Hill, when the beat of galloping hoofs sent the men scurrying to the door and out into the road.

"Our scout, Thad, reports the British are but half a mile away," the young rider gasped, as he reined in his sweat-streaked horse. Jeremiah soon learned the bearer of this news was Jonas Parker.

Captain Parker raised his big hands over his head. "Set the alarm bell to ringing," he shouted. "The British aim to get our store of arms at Concord. We haven't enough ammunition, but the Redcoats don't know that. Get your guns from the Meeting House. Line up on the green here. It's up to us to delay them until the Minutemen have time to get to Concord. To arms! To arms!"

Captain Parker turned to Jeremiah. "You had best get your horse over the stone wall yonder and ride back to Concord through the meadow."

"Yes, sir." Jeremiah gathered up Rebel's reins.

"No—wait! It's almost dawn," said Captain Parker, looking up.

The sky, Jeremiah saw, was turning a pearly lavender streaked with pink.

"Mmmm," mused the Captain. "Should you wait for sunrise you will have a faster, safer ride back, and it may be you will have good news."

Jonas Parker grinned companionably at Jeremiah. "We'll

stop those Redcoats right here in Lexington and send them running back to Boston!"

"Shall I wait then, Captain?" asked Jeremiah hopefully.

"Let him!" said young Jonas.

"All right," agreed Captain Parker, "but take cover behind the wall. A dead messenger is no good to anyone."

A chill ran up Jeremiah's spine, but he nodded and led his horse off the road.

He had thrown his coat over his nightshirt and breeches, and now as he crouched behind the stone wall he shivered, missing his warm vest and high collar. With the dawn had come a biting cold wind. It was much colder than it should be this time of year. Jeremiah rubbed his hands together. It was mid-April, he counted in his head, the nineteenth. Yes, today he would sit at Professor Parkson's desk and write on the top of his Latin paper Wednesday, April 19, 1775, that is, if the British were sent back to Boston as Captain Parker hoped. Jeremiah was almost sure they would be. According to the Captain, the British did not expect or want a fight. A patriotic show of arms would stop them.

With his arm looped through Rebel's reins, Jeremiah leaned on the stone wall and waited.

Soon he heard the rhythmic tramp of marching feet. Nearer and nearer it came. He stretched his neck. The road from Boston looked like a ribbon of scarlet. The leading company of British soldiers was almost to the village green.

Now he could see their glittering bayonets, and the gold braid of the mounted British major who led them.

Captain Parker had his men lined along the road. Soon the British would see them. Jonas stood nearest the Captain.

But, Jeremiah thought frantically, there were hundreds of Redcoats stretching down the road and no more than sixty-five or seventy Minutemen.

The scarlet-coated major pulled in his black horse and raised his hand when he saw the Minutemen. He shouted an order. Jeremiah heard the muskets rattle, the booted feet scuffle, as the rear soldiers ran forward double time to line up with those in front. "Huzza! Huzza!" they called as they ran.

The British soldiers were fanned out now and three deep. They stood straight, awaiting the major's next order.

To Jeremiah the Minutemen now looked but a handful, and he knew that many held empty guns. Yet they faced the well-armed soldiers defiantly.

Jeremiah heard Captain Parker's order to his men. "Stand your ground!" he said loudly. "Don't fire unless fired upon! But if they want a war, let it begin here!"

Seconds after the words left his lips, the British major beckoned two other mounted officers to his side. Together the three of them walked their horses slowly back and forth in front of the line of Minutemen.

"Lay down your arms, you rebels, and disperse!" the major shouted.

Some of the men stepped back, gripping their precious

muskets, but Jonas stood his ground. Jeremiah saw Captain Parker grimly wave the others forward again. True to his word he was delaying the British march to Concord.

The redcoated major was growing impatient. He spurred his horse into an angry little trot. "Lay down your arms! Why don't you lay down your arms?" he shouted.

All was suddenly still in Lexington. The sun began to rise, and to Jeremiah the silent men beyond looked like statues, or woven figures in a tapestry. Somewhere in the trees behind him a bird peeped awake. Rebel nuzzled at his shoulder, and he turned to pat her when—Zing! A shot rang out across the village green.

Who had fired it? Jeremiah could not tell. All was suddenly confusion.

One of the mounted officers shouted, "Fire! Let the rebels have it! Fire!"

The major raised his sword to stop them, but the soldiers were already raising their muskets. A volley rang out— then another!

There was a scatter of shots from the Minutemen. Jeremiah saw Jonas Parker fire, then start to reload. Before he could raise his gun to his shoulder another volley from the British rang out and Jonas fell to the ground.

Jeremiah's head reeled. There were eight dead Minutemen lying on the green. The rest had retreated into the woods, clutching their muskets. The British had not lost a single soldier.

The fifes and drums struck up a merry tune of victory as the soldiers began re-forming into lines in preparation for their march to Concord. The British major, obviously distressed, quickly glanced at the eight dead men, then dutifully trotted toward the head of the lines.

A cheer went up as another British detachment marched into Lexington. A few boisterous soldiers shot into the air, and the drums rolled louder.

Altogether, there must be almost seven hundred Redcoats now, thought Jeremiah. He must hurry, hurry back to Concord with the news.

He led Rebel deeper into the woods before he mounted. When he thought of Jonas Parker and the other men crumpled lifelessly on the ground he felt a wave of sickness, but he must hurry, hurry. The British would follow the road. The road curved. If he cut across the meadows, over fences and walls, he should reach Concord before they did.

Chapter 5

REBEL RACED across the meadows, leaping fences and fallen logs as though she had sprouted wings. In no time, it seemed, Jeremiah came upon the ridge overlooking the road from Lexington to Concord.

Captain Minot's Alarm Company of old men and boys was assembled on the ridge. When Professor Parkson called, Jeremiah reined in the lively chestnut mare, and soon he was surrounded by anxious questioning voices.

A stocky figure came running from the end of the ridge near the village where more men were gathered.

Professor Parkson turned to the newcomer and said: "Colonel Barrett, it's our messenger. He has just returned from Lexington."

"Let him speak then," the Colonel said, silencing the others with a wave of his hand. "Well, boy, what news do you bring?"

"The British are on their way," Jeremiah gasped. "About seven hundred I think, sir. They can't be more than half a mile down the road."

After he caught his breath he told what he had seen at Lexington—how the British had marched into the village

40

"The British are on their way," Jeremiah gasped.

and how Captain Parker and his men had opposed them on the triangular green.

"It was so quiet," he explained, "then there was one shot, just one shot."

"Who fired?" asked Professor Parkson.

"I could not tell, Professor. But after that it was terrible! The Redcoats fired again and again. I counted eight of our men dead, sir."

A stunned silence gripped the men about him, until in the distance down the road came the tramp, tramp, tramp of marching feet. The still moment shattered. Three of Colonel Barrett's men ran toward them along the ridge.

"They're coming, Colonel. Shall we attack from here?" asked one breathlessly.

Colonel Barrett shook his head. "No, that would be foolhardy. Our messenger has brought word they are three times our number. It's our stores of arms and ammunition they are after. We'll march over the bridge to the hills beyond, where it lies hidden, and make a stand there. Let them waste time searching the village. When more of our men arrive we'll give them a fight they will long remember, if they want it."

A cheer went up and the men began running down the ridge, across the road to the bridge. Jeremiah dismounted from his tired horse and, leading her by the reins, followed Professor Parkson.

As they hurried over the bridge toward the hills, the old Professor looked back over his shoulder and said: "I have some bread and a little cheese in my pocket. Someone must have a blanket or an extra coat. You must rest, Jeremiah."

"I'm not tired, Professor, I want to help." When he thought of the eight men lying on the ground he wanted to fight the whole British army. "I met Jonas Parker just before he was killed. Did you know him, sir?" he asked.

"Yes, I did. A good man, one of the bravest. That shot you heard in Lexington this morning, Jeremiah, will echo and re-echo. Its sound will reach everyone who believes in a government chosen by the people it governs. I spoke more truly than I knew, Jeremiah, when I said a few hours ago that we are this day living history." The old man sighed. "Ah, to be young like you, boy, when there's so much to be fought for, so much to be won, in the days ahead."

"Young!" Jeremiah exclaimed, as they reached the hill. "A boy isn't allowed—isn't able to do anything!"

"You have already brought us important information," contradicted the Professor. "Now sit here within the shelter of these trees. Here is the bread. And here is the cheese." He unwrapped a small yellow wedge and handed it to Jeremiah. "I shall see that your horse is fed and watered. Then I shall tie him near by. When I find a blanket I'll cover you. Rest, boy, we may need you again. This day has just begun."

Jeremiah nibbled at the bread and found he was very hungry. He ate the cheese too, and drank the water one of the boys brought in a tin cup. Then to please the Professor he lay on the ground, wrapped in an old ragged quilt someone had found in a barn down the road. He cradled his head on one arm and, though he protested again that he was not tired, soon fell sound asleep.

In his dreams British soldiers marched toward him. Their bayonets gleamed. Their wide belts were chalk white, their hats tall and black. As they drew closer he could see their faces, all alike. Each soldier had Roger's face. "Weavers, blacksmiths, farmers and booksellers—you are not soldiers!" they shouted in unison. "You do not know how to march. Watch us!" They halted then, and the rear soldiers ran forward double time to line up with the ones in front. "Huzza! Huzza!" they called as they ran. Their Roger faces frowned, and they raised their muskets, shouting, "Where's that boy with the horse? Where's that boy with the horse?"

Jeremiah awoke with a start. The sun was overhead. It must be noon, he thought with amazement. He looked around. Colonel Barrett was standing a few yards away, his musket over his broad shoulder. He turned to three men who were dipping their powder horns into a barrel. "Where's that boy with the horse?" he bellowed.

Jeremiah scrambled to his feet. "Here I am."

Colonel Barrett put his heavy hand on Jeremiah's shoulder. "Get something to eat at the fire over there, then meet me at the bridge. Don't forget your horse. I want you to carry extra bags of flint and ball and follow me and my men across the meadows to Merriam's Corners. That's the big farm on the road to Lexington. And listen, boy, when a man falls dead or wounded, get his powder horn. We're mighty short of gunpowder." He ran down the hill toward the bridge.

His heart beating furiously, Jeremiah ran to the open fire and dipped a ladle into the big steaming kettle of dried peas. Then Professor Parkson appeared, and while Jeremiah ate he heard the happenings of the morning. There had been a battle at the bridge about two hours ago. Two Minutemen and four Britishers had been killed.

"The British are on the run," the old Professor said. "More and more of our men are arriving all the time. Chelmsford sent over a hundred. Billerica too. Framingham sent one hundred and forty-seven and Reading's Minutemen arrived just before you awoke—two hundred and ninety of them!"

Jeremiah bolted the last of the peas. "Colonel Barrett is waiting for us, Professor," he said.

The old man stretched out his bony hand and smiled sadly. "For you, Jeremiah, not for me. Good-by, boy. I doubt we shall be studying Latin together for some time to come. This is war. Your place is with the Knoxes. They will need you. I shall send your belongings to you later on if I can."

A lump began to rise in Jeremiah's throat. "Good-by, Professor," he said with difficulty. "Thank Mrs. Parkson for me, please. You have both been so kind."

Without a backward glance he ran to Rebel, untied her reins, mounted, and trotted her briskly down the hill toward the bridge.

The last British soldier was disappearing around the ridge when Jeremiah joined Colonel Barrett.

"Now!" the Colonel shouted, raising his musket. "Across the meadows, stay out of sight. We gather at Merriam's farm."

Roger would ridicule the disorderly way the men raced across the bridge, the road, and finally behind the concealing ridge, Jeremiah decided, as he followed. Every road and path leading to Concord was filled with hurrying, angry Minutemen. Their homespun shirts and long threadbare coats flapped in the breeze as they ran. The hats they wore were of every shape and size—tricorns, round brims, and fur caps both beaver and coonskin. They carried guns and weapons of every sort—old muskets left over from the French and Indian War, broad-muzzled blunderbusses, fowling pieces that fired buckshot, short swords beaten out of farming tools, and wooden clubs. Compared to the well-armed British soldiers uniformed in tight white breeches and scarlet coats, they were a ragged crew, and, as Roger had pointed out many times, they could not march.

Marching seemed the least concern to any of them, Jeremiah decided, as he raced Rebel back across the meadows again. Most of the men had heard about Captain Parker's brave stand at Lexington and the eight deaths. They were fierce-eyed, these running rebel patriots, grimly determined to fight—and to win.

About three hundred men were gathered behind Merriam's farmhouse when Jeremiah arrived. The heavy sacks of ball and flint had rubbed the mare's neck. Her rich brown mane was matted. Jeremiah tied one flint sack and one ball sack to his own belt. Then he practiced dipping his hand in and out quickly. Once the battle began there would be no time to waste.

Deciding that his horse needed a rest, he dismounted and tied her to a tree branch.

Long strong fingers grabbed his sleeve. "You the boy with the extra flint?" a voice demanded.

Jeremiah nodded and opened his sack.

"Walker from Woburn," said the lanky young man as he took the flint.

"My name is Jeremiah Cutler. I'm from Boston," volunteered Jeremiah.

"Counting the men up ahead there must be a thousand of us by now and more acomin' all the time. Minutemen are dropping from the clouds, seems like. A bitter battle it will be, Cutler," said the young man, with a decisive shake of his head.

"Look!" exclaimed Jeremiah.

Two scarlet columns were advancing down either side of the road. No merry tune accompanied them. Their fifes and drums were still.

"Flanking parties," whispered Walker, "to protect the main body of their army on the road."

Colonel Barrett ran toward them. "Scatter! Scatter!" he shouted hoarsely. "Behind the stone walls, men, the trees. Captain Walker, get your men up ahead beyond the stream and on the other side of the road," he ordered when he spied Jeremiah's lanky companion.

"I'm off," said Captain Walker.

He put two fingers to his lips and gave a piercing whistle. A hundred men or so gathered and followed him over the stream ahead and into a grove of trees. Later on, Jeremiah knew, they would emerge from the woods and cross the road. There, others would join them from towns nearer Boston—Cambridge, Roxbury, Charlestown. Maybe Henry and William were right now on their way, and Dr. Warren too.

Now the flanking Redcoats on the near side of the road were directly in front of Merriam's farmhouse. Six of them turned suddenly, knelt, and fired. Jeremiah looked around quickly. No one had been hit.

Colonel Barrett ordered a return fire. Smoke and orange flames puffed and flashed from behind trees, walls, and fences. Two Redcoats fell and lay still. Three others appeared wounded. Two limped back to join the main army. Another dragged along on his stomach until he reached a concealing bush.

The main British army came marching down the center of the road, led by a mounted colonel and the same major who had tried without success to stop his men from firing at Lexington.

"The stout one is Colonel Smith. The other is Major Pitcairn," whispered one of the men as he snatched some balls from Jeremiah's outstretched hand. "Get along, boy; we're moving, keeping a jump ahead of them up here in the trees while they march down the road. My, they do march pretty, don't they?" He grinned. "Easy to hit, like ducks on a pond."

Astride Rebel once more, Jeremiah followed, walking his horse over the stream and into a grove of trees. Along the road to his right a narrow bridge crossed this stream. He could see the scarlet-and-white soldiers marching toward this bridge. They looked straight ahead, erect stick figures with tall black hats, lined up like ninepins. A deadly fire roared from the patriots hidden among the trees. Like ninepins the Redcoats fell. They broke ranks then, and Jeremiah could see them crowding over the narrow bridge. One fell into the stream and before he could wade ashore he was struck down.

The mounted major's scarlet sleeve waved above his running men, and his sword glittered in the early afternoon sunshine as he brandished it over their heads. His fellow officer, Colonel Smith, tried to regroup the broken army, but his commands were swallowed up by shrieks and cries. The triumphant huzzas, the merry victory tunes of a few hours before were no more. It was incredible but true, thought Jeremiah. The marching Redcoats had become a pitiful disorderly mob.

As the stricken soldiers ran along the road to Lexington, the rebel patriots kept up their fire, moving from tree to tree, fence to fence, always keeping well ahead of the astonished enemy.

The sharp smell of burnt powder stung in his nostrils, as Jeremiah rode from one demanding company to another. Immediately after the first few rounds of fire, the men had needed more balls, more flints, but most of all more gunpowder, of which he had none. He was thankful that he had not been forced to search a fallen man for his powder horn; as yet none had been killed. No doubt each newly arrived company would bring more supplies, and, as young Captain Walker had said, "they were dropping from the clouds" all the time.

They were more like clouds themselves, Jeremiah thought, these hurrying angry men, black thunderclouds growing stronger and more threatening as they gathered.

The Minutemen were moving swiftly through the trees. He followed. Soon he found himself at the exact spot where he had witnessed the Battle of Lexington. Someone had said a few minutes before that it was two o'clock. Was it possible, he thought, that so much had happened in twelve hours?

Colonel Barrett stood near the Lexington church with a group of his men. Jeremiah heeled his horse and trotted over.

"Boy," the Colonel asked, as he drew near, "did you get more powder?"

"No, sir," Jeremiah answered.

"Why not?" he asked sharply. "There have been men felled. Why not?"

The Colonel gave him no time to argue that he couldn't follow the fast-moving Minutemen and stay behind to search the fallen at the same time. The Colonel was a man with a big job on his hands. No wonder he was becoming short-tempered.

"I shall do my best, Colonel," he said.

But the Colonel was not listening. His ear was cocked

toward the road. In the distance came the clear fifed strains of "Yankee Doodle," the tune the British played to ridicule the patriots. It must be that more soldiers were on the way.

The stumbling Redcoats heard it too. Fresh troops were coming! Eagerly now they obeyed the mounted major and began to re-form into columns. They had been marching or fighting since ten o'clock the night before, Jeremiah realized. No wonder they were anxious to be rescued.

Captain Walker came running toward the church. "I've been scouting on ahead," he panted when he reached Colonel Barrett. "It's Major General Percy with 'most a thousand men—Fusiliers, Marines, the King's Own, and others. They have two cannon, fieldpieces on wheels, Colonel. They all look fresh as daisies and rarin' for a fight."

Colonel Barrett frowned. Then he said: "We'll fight back the same way as before. Pass the word to the other captains. Scatter, stay hidden, and keep well ahead of them. They won't all be able to fight us. Some will have to flank these tired troops and get them back to Boston. Now scatter, I say, and keep covered."

Jeremiah urged his horse off the road and found once more his earlier vantage spot behind the stone wall. He peered cautiously. Lord Percy's troops began marching into Lexington, still playing "Yankee Doodle."

Some Minutemen had daringly stayed grouped behind the church. Lord Percy saw them. He halted his men, lifted his sharp-nosed face and barked a command. Two soldiers stepped forward, wheeling one of the cannon onto the green. Jeremiah looked, then looked again. Yes, one of them was Roger.

The Minutemen had vanished but Lord Percy commanded the cannon to be fired nevertheless. Roger held the glowing taper. He bent over stiffly. With a deafening roar the cannon belched smoke and flame. A ball crashed through the church window.

The green was then suddenly still, as though a period of rest had been silently agreed upon by both sides. Leading Rebel by the reins, Jeremiah crept behind the wall until he reached Colonel Barrett's men who were now beyond the village, guarding the road that led to Boston.

Chapter 6

THE QUIET continued. Except for a small volley by the British and a sniping Minuteman's shot now and then, the battle seemed to have ceased. Once a dozen Redcoats, bent on revenge, ran toward Colonel Barrett's men but a roadside swamp which they had not expected stopped them. Grumbling, they returned to their companions and again all was serene.

A little after three-thirty, according to the Colonel's big gold pocket watch, Lord Percy ordered his men into marching order. Jeremiah watched as they fell into line, their sharp bayoneted muskets over their shoulders.

"Are they retreating back to Boston, Colonel?" he asked.

A voice cautioned from behind a great oak tree. "May be a trick, Colonel."

Colonel Barrett hunched his burly shoulders. "Those bayonets," he grimaced, "murderous cruel things they must be to see coming at you when you're cornered. I only hope our men stay out of barns and houses."

Captain Walker loped up. "We've got the road ahead to Boston covered on both sides, Colonel," he said. "What's your order, sir?"

The Colonel squinted shrewdly. "Let them march. We'll follow alongside as before. Keep out-of-doors, but hidden. We'll watch—see what they're up to."

It wasn't long before they saw what the British were up to. Plunder! Every house was entered. Jeremiah saw Redcoats running out of houses all the way down the road, carrying stolen goods—hams, silver bowls and candlesticks, and even bedding, patchwork quilts and feather comforters. Several of the plundered barns and houses began to smoke, then flames licked around their sides. The road to Boston was dotted with burning barns and houses. Percy made no move to stop his men.

"He aims to terrorize the countryside!" Colonel Barrett exclaimed.

A young man with his tricorn hat askew, his thin face flushed with rage, ran past Jeremiah. He clenched his fist, waved his musket, and shouted, "My sister lives down that road. She and her children have fled, but I'm not going to stand here and see her home robbed and burned!"

Disregarding his own safety he plunged from the grove of trees and into the open. He ran along the roadside. A dozen men, equally enraged, followed him.

"Fools! Fools!" the Colonel shouted. "Come back! You'll be trapped! Fools!" he shouted again as the men shot their muskets into the air in a burst of hot-headed vengeance. "Unloaded muskets against bayonets! They won't have a chance to get at their sacks of ball and powder to reload if they're seen and set upon suddenly."

But the men kept running until they came to a little

white house a few hundred yards away. Then they ran onto the road and entered the house.

"They have been seen! There's a flanking party going after them!" Jeremiah cried.

He counted fifteen Redcoats entering the house with their bayonets poised.

Shuddering, Jeremiah backed against Rebel's warm neck and covered his face with his hands. His ears rang with the cries of the bayoneted Minutemen, though he was too far away to hear them. His temples began to throb. Tears smarted his eyes. Angrily he brushed them away and forced himself to look down the road. The soldiers were leaving the house. For some reason they didn't set it afire. He counted. Every Redcoat had survived! Not one Minuteman emerged from the little white house.

Though both sides of the road swarmed with patriots, the British continued their plundering march. The losses of the Minutemen grew heavy as the furious men ran recklessly out onto the road, fired without aim, reloaded, and fired crazily again.

"Ball! Flint! Powder!" Jeremiah, still without gunpowder, answered the demands for ball and flint until his sacks were empty.

An idea formed in his mind, a terrifying one! The thirteen men had carried ammunition and he, Jeremiah, must go back for it. He would not ask permission. He would just do it!

Following the stone wall he soon was behind the little white house. Rebel whinnied and stamped as he dismounted and tied her to a fence post. "Steady, girl, steady," he whispered, patting her nose. "You'll be safe here behind this barn."

Carrying his empty sacks he crept around the side of the house. He entered through the open door. It was deathly still inside. In his mind he had planned what he would do. He would not look at the brave silent men, only grope for their powder horns and ammunition sacks which they would be glad to give him if they could.

With his eyes half-closed he managed to do just that. His sacks were soon full, but he had not finished gathering up all the ammunition. Rebel, he remembered, had an empty bag swinging on her saddle. He must get it.

"Sssh, there may be a stray Redcoat about," he cautioned his whinnying mare, as he tied the full sacks to her saddle and tucked the empty one under his arm.

Again he crept around the side of the house.

"Halt!" The stern command was followed by a sharp jab between his shoulder blades. Dropping the bag, he raised his hands over his head.

"About face!" the voice commanded.

Jeremiah turned to find Roger confronting him. With a startled cry Roger lowered his musket and stared.

"Jeremiah," he said after a moment, "what are you doing here?"

"Fighting Redcoats!" Jeremiah answered grimly.

Roger laughed. He adjusted his tall leather hat and tugged at his tight white vest, as though he hoped Jeremiah would take note of his splendid uniform, his scarlet coat with its green-faced lapels.

"Really," he said with a sly smile, "you are amusing. Fighting, you say? Where are your weapons?"

What a temptation it was to brag about the ammunition sacks tied to Rebel's saddle. He must not. If Roger knew, he would capture them, and probably Rebel too. Jeremiah offered a little prayer, "Please, God, don't let Rebel whinny or stamp."

Roger began talking. "We have had a difficult time getting here, Lord Percy and I, and our men, of course," he said haughtily. "At Cambridge the planks were off the bridge and stacked by the side of the road. That delayed us. Then, would you believe it, we had just started when twelve old men led by a half-breed Indian dumped our supply wagons! But we did arrive, as you see, my friend, and soon just punishments will be meted out to all."

It was hard to hold back an angry retort, but silence was wisest.

"How happy I am that you are unarmed, Jeremiah," Roger continued, with another smirk. "How I should hate to claim a half-grown boy, a bookseller's sweeper boy at that, my only prisoner. It might make a bad impression. What's more I should have to share the horse I st—borrowed with you. He's waiting under a tree just ahead. Too bad, my boy. You shall have to trudge all the way back to Boston."

With a wave of his hand he turned smartly on his heel and walked down the road. Soon he was out of sight.

Relieved after his narrow escape, Jeremiah decided against re-entering the house. It would be foolish to risk the ammunition he already had. The quicker it reached patriotic hands the better.

The running, marching, mobile battle had reached Cambridge before Jeremiah caught up with it. The Minutemen had increased in numbers. They swarmed among the trees and onto the road, boldly attacking Lord Percy's rear guard, quickly smothering the soldiers' feeble flanking maneuvers.

Nowhere could Jeremiah find Colonel Barrett. All was confusion. He questioned men he passed—men from Brookline, Malden, Roxbury, Beverly, Dedham, and other towns near Boston—all had sent their Minutemen to meet Lord Percy.

A toothless old man chuckled in Jeremiah's ear. "We wanted to be sure the British got back into that nice little trap they made out of Boston."

"Boston! My friends are there! They have a bookstore on Cornhill." He grabbed the old man's arm. "What happened to the people of Boston?"

"There, there now," the old man said soothingly. "Your friends are patriotic rebels, I take it? Well then, they probably got out long ago. Most likely they're fighting somewhere about. There are lots here from Boston. See, there's Dr. Warren over there." He pointed to a tall figure standing on a slope a few yards away.

"Dr. Warren!" shouted Jeremiah trotting Rebel toward the slope.

"It is Jeremiah Cutler; yes, of course," the doctor said with a tired smile. His collar was torn, his face smudged with grime.

"Oh, Dr. Warren, this is no time to bother you, but—"

"Henry is around here somewhere," Dr. Warren said with an understanding nod. "Lucy is snug and safe at a friend's house in Watertown. The Ballards left a week ago so your friend Sam is safe too." He hesitated. "But I regret to tell you that William Knox is trapped in Boston."

"Oh, no!"

"Now don't worry. We must hope and pray for the best. William is a bright lad. He'll find a way to get out."

Jeremiah sighed.

"It has been a brave battle, Jeremiah," Dr. Warren continued. "The British are beaten for the time being. But had we a commander in chief we could drive them into their ships and out of the harbor. As it is we are separated into little bands. There is no one to organize these spirited men."

Strange, Jeremiah thought, Henry had said the same thing not so long ago: "If we fight, we shall need a leader, one who will command the respect and loyalty of all."

Dr. Warren nudged him. "If that's ammunition you're carrying, Jeremiah, distribute it. We need it!"

"Yes, sir!"

He answered the shouts of "Ball! Flint! Powder!" until again his supplies ran out. But by that time the last of Major General Percy's army had straggled into Boston, either by way of the Neck or the Bay. Into the trap they marched, the trap they had so carefully prepared for the rebels.

The American camps were to be spread in a half circle

around Boston, from Roxbury to Chelsea, Jeremiah learned.

Henry Knox, the bookseller, someone said, would be easy to find. He was at the center of the half circle in Cambridge. A big house opposite Harvard College was being used as American Headquarters. General Artemas Ward had been placed temporarily in command and Henry, as a Boston Grenadier lieutenant, was assigned to artillery.

The sun was setting as Jeremiah guided his tired horse along the cobbled Cambridge street. The tall college buildings just ahead were bathed in a rosy glow. Wearily he smiled at a little private joke. He had always wanted to go to Harvard. Now here he was!

Chapter 7

Ticonderoga. Ticonderoga. By the end of May the men assembled in Cambridge spoke of little else. Because of the different war committees of the separate colonies, two men had been ordered to lead the attack on the British fortress, Ethan Allen and Benedict Arnold.

"Who did capture Ticonderoga from the British?" Jeremiah asked Henry. They were sitting on a ruined lawn near the college, chewing laboriously on their noonday rations of dried beef. William, they had heard with relief, was safe but still unable to get through the lines.

"Both," answered Henry, "Arnold for Connecticut, and Ethan Allen's Green Mountain Boys for the Vermont territory. So Captain Brown reports. Not a man was killed on either side. It was a task well done by both men, but the waste of it! Two companies, two able leaders!"

"There are thousands of cannon balls, almost a hundred fieldpieces," Jeremiah commented. "All sorts of valuable stores up there, so they say."

Henry looked off into the distance toward Boston, as though he could see the British encamped on the beautiful

Common. "How we could use them here to blast the Red-coats out of Boston," he said.

"Transport them three hundred miles or more!"

"It could be done. I would try if I had the authority," Henry declared, rising to his feet. "If only there were some leader to appeal to. Each colony committee plans in a different direction. It makes hard feelings. Let's hope the Continental Congress in Philadelphia settles the matter of a commander in chief once and for all."

"Perhaps Colonel Arnold will find a way to bring the artillery back." Jeremiah remembered well the short but imposing figure of Arnold in his scarlet Connecticut uniform. He had heard Captain Brown say that the prosperous young merchant, Arnold, loved money too well, but it would never do to repeat it to Henry. Henry strongly disapproved of malicious gossip.

"Benedict Arnold transport that artillery? Never! He is already disgruntled, and rightly so, because he has been reduced to second in command of the Connecticut troops. Besides," said Henry, "he is obsessed with the idea of capturing Quebec."

"Quebec! Is that near Lake Champlain too?"

"No, Jeremiah, but it can be reached from the lake. Look," he picked up a stick and began to draw in the sun-dried earth. "Here is Quebec, directly north of Boston, about two hundred miles overland, a trip easy for a bird but not for a man. The country is rugged. By water, however, Quebec is easily reached. Arnold is an extremely able military man. His plan may be a two-pronged attack, one from Boston by way of the ocean and Kennebec River, and one from the west by way of Lake Champlain, the Richelieu and St. Lawrence rivers."

"But the freezing weather?"

"Of course, boy, a winter attack would be impossible. Even in November Canada is bitter with ice and snow," Henry agreed.

"Never mind the attack. What about Ticonderoga?" Jeremiah said impatiently. Henry had praised his bravery at Lexington and Concord. But as the days passed he forgot. Once again Jeremiah was treated like a child.

As two men approached Jeremiah sprang to his feet.

"Yes, what about Ticonderoga, son?" said the older, a rough, hard-bitten man with a Southern drawl.

Jeremiah was delighted to see Henry blush like a schoolboy.

"Colonel John Stark from New Hampshire and Israel Putnam from Connecticut have been telling me about this Ticonderoga," the homespun-clad man continued. He gripped his gun in both hands. It was over five feet in length and very slender, a gun such as Jeremiah had never seen before. "A rifle, son," drawled the older man in answer to Jeremiah's questioning look. "I'm Jim Thompson of Dan Morgan's riflemen. Was here visiting when the fur began to fly. If this war gets agoing you'll see more rifles like this and old Dan Morgan himself. I betcha."

The rifleman blinked and scratched behind his ear. Then he turned to his companion. "Boys, this young'un here is Nathan Hale, a schoolteacher from Connecticut. Quite a mix-up we got here in Cambridge, eh?"

"Former schoolteacher," smilingly corrected the good-looking young man at Thompson's side. "Until we regain our rights I intend to stay with the Knowlton Rangers." He bowed and smiled again as Henry introduced himself and Jeremiah.

"I stand corrected," Thompson said with a good-natured, growling laugh. "Now, son," he said, tapping Henry's heavy shoulder, "get on with your geography lesson. I fought long and hard in the French and Indian War, but never did hit this Fort Ticonderoga everyone's talking about. Where is it exactly? What's it like? Putnam, the old rogue, just looks wise and says, 'At Ticonderoga a man finds what stuff he's made of. Ticonderoga measures a man.' What's so special 'bout this place?"

"I have never been there," said young Nathan Hale, turning his clear blue eyes on Jeremiah, "but I can visualize the mountains, the sparkling lake water. A quiet spot of beauty, it must be, where a man would naturally turn to deep soul-searching thoughts."

"We're not all such lofty thinkers, Nathan," said the Virginia rifleman with gruff affection. "On with it now," he said, indicating Henry's scratches in the dirt with the toe of his dusty boot.

"I have never been to the fort or to Lake Champlain," admitted Henry sheepishly, "but I shall tell you what I know." His pointed stick moved in the dirt once more. "It's a long, long lake, from north to south over a hundred miles, and almost five hundred square miles in area, so they say. It has rapids in some places and swamps in others, and a great many islands, one twelve miles in length.

Beyond its western shores in New York are the Adirondack Mountains, and to the east the Green Mountains."

"Ethan Allen's country," interrupted Jeremiah eagerly, picturing the Green Mountain Boys embarking in canoes to storm the fort. Allen, he had heard, wore a strange uniform of his own design, a green coat with huge fringed gold shoulder ornaments and bright yellow breeches. His cousin, Ebenezer Allen, was said to engage in a private war over and beyond winning Vermont's independence from New York and fighting the British. Slavery enraged him and any Negro slave that he captured he set free, after writing out a legal-looking document of emancipation in a bold, firm hand. Some would call this disorganization, Jeremiah knew, but to others it was the same fight, the fight for freedom.

Henry seemed a little annoyed at the interruption. "Yes, yes, Allen's country," he said. "Now, here, about twenty-five miles north of the southern tip of Champlain and lying west of it, is another lake, much smaller, only thirty miles long. It's called Lake George. These two lakes are joined by a thin stream which curves around Sugar Loaf Mountain, some call it Mt. Defiance. On Champlain's western bank at this stream's beginning is Fort Ticonderoga. So you can see what an important point it is. If the British still held the fort they could sweep down Lake George to the Hudson River, and eventually cut off New England and New York from the rest of the colonies."

"Mighty important," agreed Thompson, mopping his weather-beaten brow with a big red kerchief. "Knox makes a good teacher, eh, Nathan?" he added with a droll wink.

"Excellent," agreed the young Connecticut Ranger. "I understand," he said to Henry, "that one of these British generals lately arrived in Boston fought near Ticonderoga during the French and Indian War."

"Yes, you mean General Howe. He did, and his older brother was killed at Quebec in that war. In fact, we have in Boston a monument to the late George Howe."

"How very strange," mused the tall young man named Hale. "War twists lives into unforeseen patterns."

The former schoolteacher looked so sad that suddenly Jeremiah wanted to make his handsome face crinkle with laughter.

"Have you heard the verse that is being told about, since the three new British generals arrived in Boston Harbor on the ship *Cerberus*? It goes like this:

"Behold the Cerberus the Atlantic plough
Her precious cargo Burgoyne, Clinton, Howe
Bow-wow-wow!"

Thompson and Hale threw back their heads and laughed. Henry's jolly laugh rang out too. Then he nudged his young former apprentice as though he wished to speak in confidence with his fellow soldiers and said, "Hadn't you better get some hay for your horse, Jeremiah?"

Jeremiah felt his face growing red with embarrassment at being sent off like a too-talkative child, but he drew himself up proudly, said good-by, and left.

The hastily assembled camps beyond the college were

always interesting to see. As he passed them, he noted again the neat tents made of ship sails. They sheltered the Marblehead fishermen. Others were not so trim and orderly. There were turf huts, ramshackle lean-tos, and shelters thrown together out of twigs and driftwood. The truest rebel patriot, Jeremiah thought, would have to admit that the American Army was oddly assorted.

Rebel stamped and snorted when he approached. Jeremiah patted her nose and put his cheek against her soft reddish mane. He thought again of the wild ride they had taken nearly six weeks before. A new Patriots' Day had been born that day, everyone said. In the future, Dr. Warren would address the people on April 19 instead of March 5.

Jeremiah hadn't talked to Dr. Warren since. The doctor was busy with the Provincial Congress. He traveled to Philadelphia frequently to confer with John Hancock and the Adams cousins who were sitting with the Second Continental Congress. Dr. Warren would laugh at that verse about Clinton, Burgoyne, and Howe. He must remember to tell the doctor the next time he saw him.

But Jeremiah never saw Dr. Warren again.

On Monday evening, June 18, Jeremiah returned from escorting Lucy to Worcester. Henry had insisted upon it. It had been mercilessly hot for three days. Rebel's flanks were lathered from the heat when Jeremiah rode into Cambridge just after sundown.

Distraught, Henry came to meet him. "Bad news, Jeremiah," he mumbled.

"Is it William?"

"No. William is safe. A deserting British soldier brought me a letter from him. He has been allowed to keep the bookstore and has decided to stay as long as he can. It is only a matter of time before martial law is declared and all our property confiscated. I hope William does not tarry too long. I'll try to get word to him. But there is bad news, boy. Dismount and sit with me under this tree."

It was then that Jeremiah learned how terrible the battle had been on the hills about Charlestown, Breed's Hill and Bunker's. The village itself lay in smoldering ashes.

"The British lost twice as many men as we did," Henry said, "including Major Pitcairn who vowed to his last breath that he did not order his men to fire at Lexington. Our loss, Jeremiah, was very great. We lost Dr. Warren."

Dr. Warren! Jeremiah buried his face in his hands.

Finally he raised his head and said accusingly, "You knew about this Bunker Hill battle. That's why you sent me away. Dr. Warren didn't treat me so. I was one of his messengers. I should have been here to help him."

"I'm sorry, Jeremiah. Truly I am. Everyone feels as you do about Dr. Warren. He will be sorely missed."

"Henry, I want to train with the Home Guard. I am going to! Even if it's only a regiment of old men and boys, a last-resort regiment."

Henry looked startled for a moment, then he said slowly: "Very well, boy. If both your mother and mine were alive I guess they would understand. I shall speak to General Ward tomorrow."

Scarcely two weeks later, on July 2, Jeremiah trotted Rebel leisurely along the dry dusty road outside of the Cambridge limits. He had been drilling all morning. He now knew how to load a musket swiftly. A British soldier, said the other militia men, had to follow a dozen distinct orders to load and fire his gun. The first shouted command meant bite the end off the paper cartridge which contained the ball and powder. The second command, shake some powder into the musket's pan. The third, close lid of pan. The fourth, drop gun butt to ground. Fifth, pour rest of powder into barrel. Sixth, jiggle gun to settle powder. Seventh, put in ball. Eighth, cram in paper. Ninth, ram it down. Tenth, raise loaded musket. Eleventh, aim! Twelfth, fire!!

The Americans were told to "Prime, load, and fire!" If the powder just flashed in the pan and failed to eject the ball, they were expected to use their wits and reload as fast as possible.

Jeremiah had no uniform, though he had more clothes than many others, since Professor Parkson had managed to send his trunk to him. And he had no money. He soon used his last shilling for food. Food was scarce, but cloth was scarcer. It was impossible to tell the colonels from the majors, and the majors from the captains, since each man clothed himself as best he could. This was sometimes disconcerting. On the other hand, as Jeremiah's very young bunk mate said: "The Britishers spend half a day just keeping their brass polished, their boots blacked, their hair greased and braided. Wonder how they manage those curls in front of their ears." Jeremiah had laughed and answered, "Glue!"

Thinking of it he laughed again as he continued down the dusty road. Rebel's smooth gait was relaxing. He soon found himself giving the chestnut mare her head. Let her set the pace and pick the path, he thought drowsily.

Suddenly the mare stopped short. She pranced. Her ears twitched. Jeremiah listened. The rhythmic beat of horses in cavalcade drew nearer and nearer.

He wheeled his horse off the road. Could it be General George Washington himself? The new Commander in Chief had left Philadelphia only ten days ago. No doubt he would be asked to speak in every town he passed. It was known he had stopped in Manhattan and taken leave there of General Philip Schuyler. Schuyler, who was called the Albany Patroon because of his Dutch ancestry and huge holdings on the Hudson River, had been given command of the Northern Army, including the troops at Ticonderoga. Was it possible that the approaching cavalcade brought General Washington? If so, he was arriving much sooner than expected.

Jeremiah waited, reining in his horse beside a big tree. He remembered how Henry had fairly bounced with joy when news came of the Continental Congress' choice for Commander in Chief of the Continental Army. "When General George Washington arrives we shall have an organized army," he had declared, his eyes bright with conviction, "and the King will soon restore our charter and rightful government."

Henry never spoke of independence, the way Samuel Adams and many others did. And, according to what Jeremiah had heard, neither did George Washington.

The hoofbeats grew louder. Now he could hear voices. Soon he saw the tricorn hats of two riders, then two more. He quieted the stamping Rebel.

Several uniformed soldiers on horseback passed by. Their sheathed swords slapped against their thighs as they rode. Then came three riders, flanked by more mounted soldiers. Jeremiah stretched his neck to see the three men. Only one could be George Washington. The tall straight rider astride a big bay horse must be the new Commander in Chief.

As the General rode past, Jeremiah had a fleeting impression of a pale face, a large straight nose, tightly closed lips, and a firm chin. The big man was magnificent.

Jeremiah urged Rebel a little nearer the road. General Washington's uniform, he saw, was buff and blue. Beneath his black hat his white wig was clubbed and tied at the nape of his neck. Jeremiah marveled at the ease with which the General sat his horse. His big hands held the reins loosely, confidently. His long booted legs hugged the bay's sides as though they belonged there. The General and his horse were one.

Henry had recounted that George Washington owned a big plantation in Virginia, and rode from dawn until dusk overseeing his farms. For recreation, he hunted the fox with his hounds. No wonder he seemed a part of his horse.

Jeremiah could imagine Roger's first words when he heard of the new American general. "Indeed. Now the weavers, blacksmiths, millers, and booksellers, have a farmer-fox hunter to lead them. How amusing!" But perhaps Roger had changed his low estimate of the part-time American soldiers by now.

Before the rest of the cavalcade passed, Rebel was turned around, urged deeper into the trees and bushes. There was a shorter way back to Cambridge, a narrow dirt path. Jeremiah guided his horse onto it and heeled her into a canter. Henry would want to know. The devotion once lavished on his books seemed of late directed toward the General he had never seen. Jeremiah hoped his friend and former employer would not be disillusioned when he met his hero in person. As for himself, impressed though he was by the erect buff-and-blue figure on horseback, no one, he vowed, would ever quite measure up to Dr. Warren.

Chapter 8

As THE WEEKS went by it became apparent to Jeremiah that Henry Knox had not been disillusioned. His admiration for the tall serious Commander in Chief deepened with each passing day. "If the General asked Henry to swim to England and capture the King, he would try it," joked Thompson, the Virginia rifleman.

Thompson was proud of his fellow Virginian, George Washington, but even more proud of Dan Morgan who had arrived in August with over fourteen hundred crackshot riflemen from Virginia, Pennsylvania, and Maryland.

During the early summer, while he waited impatiently for old Dan Morgan, the gruff Thompson had amused himself by teaching Jeremiah rifle marksmanship. The rifle, the boy found, was harder to load but deadly accurate.

Early in September, Thompson presented him with one of the long slender weapons as a parting gift. As Jeremiah thanked him, the hard-bitten Virginian said gruffly, "No thanks necessary, son. Someday I might need you to defend me."

Jeremiah thought this very unlikely but he said, "If that day ever comes, I shall try to remember all you have taught me." He gripped the rifle proudly. "You are off to Quebec I hear, sir."

"Yep. Told you things would start popping once Dan Morgan got here," he said, with his peculiar growling laugh. "We're agoing with Benedict Arnold and his men. Marching up to Newburyport. We embark there, cross the ocean to the mouth of the Kennebec River. Hear the New York troops are leaving Ticonderoga. They aim to take St. Johns and Montreal by way of Lake Champlain and the rivers up north there."

"The Richelieu and the St. Lawrence?" Jeremiah asked, remembering the map Henry had drawn in the dirt.

"Yep, yep. Just like folks have been asaying. It'll be a two-pronged attack on Canada. Montgomery's leading the New York troops 'cause General Schuyler's attending some Indian Council in Albany." Thompson pulled off his hat and scratched his head. "What tribes they got up there?" he asked.

"The Six Nations of the Iroquois—Mohawks, Oneidas, Onondagas, Cayugas, Senecas, and Tuscaroras," Jeremiah answered, frowning as he tried to pronounce each name correctly. "They stretch across the north, from above Albany to the west beyond New York territory, I think."

"Like a big scythe, eh? Sure hope they go along with us or stay neutral," Thompson said, scratching his head again before he replaced his hat. "Anyway, could be we'll run over to help Montgomery and his Yorkers with Montreal about mid-October. Dan Morgan will chase Guy Carleton and his Redcoats out of Quebec in a week."

"Before the cold sets in?" Jeremiah asked cautiously, wondering whether Virginians could imagine the bitter cold of a Canadian winter.

"Sure, sure. Dan don't waste time. That Arnold fella looks to know what he's about too. Small, but cocky, and brave too, his men say. 'By, son. Could be we'll meet again."

"I hope so, sir," said Jeremiah, shifting the new rifle to his shoulder as he grasped the strong rough hand.

After the Quebec expedition left, the camps seemed uncomfortably quiet. There were skirmishes now and then between the Americans and the redcoated sentries at Boston Neck. The Americans took pleasure in tormenting the British until they fired a volley. Then they ran from their hiding places and gathered up the balls for their own use. In spite of these breaks in camp life monotony, the noisy good humor of the riflemen was missed.

After General Washington's arrival, the American Continental Army became an organized body. Though Congress had no funds for uniforms, Washington ingeniously devised an inexpensive method of distinguishing one rank from another. The Commander in Chief himself wore a wide light-blue ribbon across his chest. His major generals wore purple, his brigadier generals pink. Colonels wore green. The field officers wore feathers of different colors in their hats—yellow, red, or green—and the sergeants wore red shoulder knots, the corporals green. The men were no longer called militia or Minutemen. They were now soldiers of the Continental Army.

Jeremiah, as a member of the Cambridge Home Guard, was a militia man. He wore a loose tan shirt of homespun over his breeches, which he belted tightly at the waist. Many of his fellow guardsmen had no such uniform, but during the summer Lucy had somehow managed to find enough cloth to make a shirt. He wore the same old black hat he had worn to Concord the preceding spring, only now it was turned up into a tricorn.

By early November, two months after the Quebec expedition left Cambridge, Jeremiah proudly stuck a green feather in his tricorn hat. He was a field officer in the Home Guard Militia. He had long ago stripped the buckles from his shoes because, as every militia man knew, a glittering buckle could betray its owner's hiding place.

At fifteen, Jeremiah had become a fairly good marksman. His rifle was envied by all, even Henry. Of late, though, he rarely saw his former protector. Henry was encamped at Roxbury. Neither had Jeremiah heard any news about William, except that he was now finding it difficult to get out of Boston, for martial law had been declared. He was surprised and overjoyed, therefore, early one morning to see William riding toward him.

Jeremiah was standing in front of his quarters, an old barn at the edge of town, when William arrived. After feeding Rebel, the boy had filled his own bunk with fresh straw and donned his militia garb in preparation for morning drill. Just before William rode up he had been deciding whether to wear his coat, thereby covering his militia shirt, or to brave the raw chilling sweep of November's wind. He had about decided in favor of the warm coat, but William's unexpected approach and their joyful reunion sent his thoughts scattering.

They thumped each other's backs and jumped around, laughing. They both talked at once, asking one question after another. The bookstore had been looted and left a shambles. "But we shall get it back soon," William vowed. His face grew feverishly pink as he admired Jeremiah's rifle and inspected his quarters.

"I must not forget why I came!" he exclaimed suddenly. "General Washington wants to see you right away!"

Jeremiah's knees began to shake. "See me?" he asked incredulously.

"Don't look so scared. Get your horse, and I shall tell you all about it on the way."

"Henry," William explained as they rode, "is a colonel, although his commission papers haven't come through yet. General Washington is sending him to Ticonderoga to get artillery. He, the General, says we may go too, if we are as capable as Henry said we are. You see, Henry is being allowed expenses for two servants. What do you think of that? Come on, Jeremiah! Heel your horse. We must not keep General Washington waiting!"

With his heart beating as fast as Rebel's hoofs, Jeremiah rode side by side with William toward the new headquarters on Brattle Street in Cambridge. "Ticonderoga measures a man, that's what they said." Jeremiah gave his whistling nineteen-year-old friend a quick side glance. Was Henry's hero worship of the new Commander in Chief leading the three of them into an impossible task? The scheme for transporting the cannon from Ticonderoga to Boston had long been brewing in Henry's mind, and Jeremiah did not doubt that he had begged for the mission. "Ticonderoga in midwinter," he thought, frowning at its ominous sound, but another glance at William's happy, confident profile banished his misgivings. Here was his opportunity to help free Boston. Suddenly he was determined to go. "Henry had better not change his mind. I am going!"

But in the end, he knew, it would be General Washington's decision. As they approached the graceful doorway of Vassal House Jeremiah's courage wavered, not at the thought of Ticonderoga in midwinter, but of the impending interview. If only Dr. Warren sat behind those closed doors, he thought, after a blue-jacketed Marbleheader stopped them at the door and then showed them into the hall.

As they stood waiting, Jeremiah confided his fears to his friend. "I am very uneasy about this meeting. General Washington always looks so grim."

William whispered back solemnly, "Henry says the General has reason to be grim, especially of late. Do you remember Nathanael Greene?"

"The man in Rhode Island we used to send books to?"

"The very same. He and Henry have become good friends. Greene is here in Cambridge in command of the Rhode Island troops. Just a few weeks ago he uncovered a traitorous spy among us, none other than Dr. Church of

Boston. All of our secret information has been going to the British. This was a terrible blow to General Washington. Then, the rumor has reached us that the King is hiring Hessians to fight against us. Think what that would mean."

Jeremiah began to understand. "There has been some good news, though," he said. "The Marbleheaders have captured some food supplies and some arms too from British cargo ships. And Montgomery has taken St. Johns in Canada."

"Yes, that's true. And, of course, when Benjamin Franklin arrived a few weeks ago to reassure General Washington of Congress' full confidence in him, it must have helped."

"Still," Jeremiah insisted, "I wish the General didn't look so tight-lipped."

William chuckled softly. "Some say he tightens his lips to keep his temper under control, though Henry claims he has never seen him anything but calm. But others say he does it to fight the pain of his continuously aching teeth."

Jeremiah's fears fled. William's explanations had made the erect buff-and-blue figure seem very human. He could grasp now some idea of the burdensome task before the new Commander in Chief who, through it all, must also suffer the doubts, disillusionments, pains, and weaknesses of ordinary men.

When the big doors swung wide and a Negro servant smiled and bade them enter, Jeremiah followed his friend in a respectful but fearless frame of mind.

Chapter 9

As JEREMIAH drew closer to the big man seated at a mahogany table, he saw that General George Washington had one victory to his credit that William had failed to mention. The white-wigged head was bent over a document, but the deeply pitted skin on his high cheekbones revealed a long-ago battle with the dreaded smallpox, a battle for life, fought and won.

The high-ceilinged room smelled pleasantly of hot sealing wax and lemon-oil floor polish. A trace of tobacco smoke from some previous visitor still lingered in the room.

A curtain behind the General suddenly billowed, and the Negro servant rushed over and closed the window, muttering about drafts bringing rheumatism.

"Thank you, Timmy," said the General as the servant left the room. Then he looked up.

"General Washington," said William, "may I present my brother's young apprentice, Jeremiah Cutler?"

The General nodded at Jeremiah unsmilingly, then said to William, "Billy, you and Harry will leave for New York on the sixteenth."

"Yes, sir," William answered eagerly.

Jeremiah was surprised to hear the Knox brothers called Billy and Harry. But then he remembered hearing that General Washington had nicknames for those close to him. He was proud that his friends had won the trust of the new Commander in Chief.

"Harry is working over his plans in the room across the hall," General Washington continued. "You may be able to do some writing for him, Billy. Go now and see."

Bursting with enthusiasm William dashed toward the door. Jeremiah started to follow, but the General's next words stopped him.

"Young Cutler," he said, "one moment."

Jeremiah turned to find the General's gaze upon him. The door closed after William, leaving him terribly alone. The polished floor and expanse of carpet between him and the seated figure seemed to lengthen as the General beckoned him closer.

"Young Cutler, have you ever been north?"

"No, sir," Jeremiah answered.

"Have you ever been without food and warmth for any length of time?" the General continued.

"No, sir, not really," he admitted.

"Have you ever seen Mohawk Indians in war paint?" the General persisted.

"No, General Washington," he said, controlling his quivering voice with difficulty.

"Do you know that Colonel Knox has volunteered to perform an almost impossible task?" the Virginian asked, dropping his glance to the papers before him.

"Almost impossible, sir, but Henry, the Colonel, is most capable, sir."

The General looked up with startling suddenness. "Do you, young man, want to go with him?" he asked.

"Yes, sir!"

"Why?" bluntly demanded the General.

"We have to drive the British out of Boston, sir," Jeremiah said. Then, forgetting his timidity, he repeated urgently, "We have to! We need the guns at Ticonderoga to do it. I want to help Henry get them. But it isn't only because of that." The General's face remained expressionless but Jeremiah went on. "You see, sir, after Dr. Warren was killed at Bunker Hill I—well, I promised myself I would help free Boston if I could. Maybe I am not so brave or smart as some, sir, but if I am allowed to go to Ticonderoga I shall do what I'm told and help Colonel Knox and his brother all I can. Please give your permission, General Washington."

The Virginian did not answer. He stood up and walked to the window. "I have been too bold." Jeremiah chided himself for talking about Ticonderoga, Boston, and Dr. Warren all in one breath. What a disconnected plea he had made, beyond anyone's understanding!

He watched General Washington pull aside the curtain and study the bare November trees outside and he thought, "I have spoiled everything."

"You were fond of Dr. Warren?" the General asked finally, still gazing out the window.

"Most fond, sir," Jeremiah said, thinking that the General did seem to understand after all.

Was he to go to Ticonderoga or not?

General Washington seated himself once more behind the table. He looked up and nodded. "That will be all," he said.

Jeremiah backed toward the door uncertainly. Was he to go to Ticonderoga or not?

The tight-lipped Virginian watched as Jeremiah stumbled over the carpet edge. Then he nodded again and said, "Well, Jeremy, get along. Don't delay. Arrange leave with your militia captain. You and the Knox brothers will be gone for two months or longer."

In a daze Jeremiah stepped out into the hall and bumped into a thin uniformed figure. As he apologized, he recognized the sullen face of General Charles Lee. Even the reprimand Lee uttered sharply did not dampen his delirious joy. "He called me Jeremy," he thought. "That means he likes me, he trusts me! And I can go to Ticonderoga!" He hurried across the hall to tell the good news.

By the sixteenth of November all arrangements had been made. Henry had examined the artillery in the camps around Boston as the General had ordered and was ready to proceed to Manhattan. There he was to present General Washington's request to New York's Provincial Congress that they send to Cambridge immediately as many small arms as they could spare.

They would use the post road along the coast, William told Jeremiah, as they made last-minute preparations and waited for Henry to return from his farewell visit to Lucy in Worcester.

Jeremiah strapped his small trunk behind his saddle. He

found his long rifle a problem to pack. Finally he slipped the long slender barrel through his stirrup strap and tied the butt to his saddle with a leather thong.

William's face was flushed with excitement. He coughed, then quickly covered his mouth with his hand, as though his brother might hear and forbid him to go on the arduous northern journey.

"Did you put General Greene's letters in Henry's saddlebag, Jeremiah?" he asked. "We are to leave his packet of mail at a Rhode Island farmhouse to be forwarded."

"Yes, and my own bag is half-filled with other letters. When it got about we were leaving, almost everyone with friends or relatives along our route wanted to send one." He thought it must be nice to receive a letter. He never had.

"We shall take them all, even if we have to carry them in our hats." William laughed boyishly.

By the time Henry returned from Worcester, the boys were eager to start.

All the way down, Jeremiah, or Jeremy, as the Knoxes now called him teasingly, feared he would have to exchange Rebel for a fresh horse. In Connecticut both Henry and William were forced to exchange theirs. But though the chestnut mare tired toward the end of the day, a night's rest revived her to fresh liveliness each morning.

They reached New York on Saturday, November 25, and found lodgings on King Street, between City Hall and the French church.

During the next three days, while Henry conferred with the Provincial Congress, William and Jeremiah rode about the city, which Henry had warned them was "full of Tories."

They stopped at the Merchant's Coffee House where public notices were posted. It was there, amidst an excited group of arm-waving men, that they learned Montreal had been taken by Montgomery, but that Ethan Allen had been captured by the British.

They trotted down Broadway to the fort on the southern tip of Manhattan Island. They visited the Fly Market on Maiden Lane. Jeremiah thought it a queer name for a place where all sorts of produce were sold.

On their way back up Broadway they passed brick houses which William said were in the Dutch style because the Dutch had been the first to settle New York. Beyond their lodging house was Fresh Pond, and they stopped to see the pumps which supplied the city with water. Still farther north was King's College, which they decided could not compare to Harvard.

"I like New York," said Jeremiah as he rubbed down Rebel. Henry had accomplished his mission and they were preparing to leave for the north. "I like the coffee houses. In fact, I think when I come of age I shall open a combination bookstore and coffee house right here in Manhattan."

Henry raised his eyebrows. William stopped buckling the strap on his saddle and stared at him.

"Why not Boston?" they asked in unison.

"I wouldn't want to take customers away from your bookstore after you've been so kind to me," Jeremiah explained.

Henry and William threw back their heads and laughed. Jeremiah couldn't help joining in.

"Well, Jeremy," Henry declared, "you have plenty of time to decide."

"I was fifteen on October 9," Jeremiah reminded him.

"Soon you will have a beard," teased William.

They all laughed again. Then Henry admitted that he liked New York better than he had expected. He had been pleasantly surprised by the number and determination of New York patriots. "Though they do talk too fast."

"A small fault," commented William.

"Small, yes." A twinkle came in his brother's eye, "when you consider that they cast their own cannon right here in the city and have agreed to send twelve good iron four-pounders with shells and shot to Cambridge immediately."

"When will we reach Ticonderoga?"

"It's Albany first, boy," Henry answered, "to see General Schuyler, the Commander of the Northern Army."

William said thoughtfully: "I wonder if there are places along the Hudson River where we can get lodging and fresh horses?"

"There will be farmhouses willing to take us in," Henry said. "As for the horses, they should last until we reach Albany. I hope we'll be there by the first of December."

Jeremiah sighed with relief. He could not bear to think of handing Rebel over to some stranger.

They crossed the river by ferry and approached General

Schuyler's hilltop house on December 2, a day later than Henry had expected.

Rebel held out, but Jeremiah knew he could press her no further. She had begun to limp badly.

Reluctantly he decided, as they trotted up the road that wound its way to the Schuyler Mansion, that he and Rebel must part.

Chapter 10

BEHIND THE red-brick Schuyler house were barns, smoke-houses, and long white buildings which housed the General's indentured servants and slaves. The Schuylers had another mansion and many acres of farm land farther up the Hudson, north of Saratoga.

"Wait here with the horses, Jeremy," Henry said, after they had dismounted near one of the barns behind the mansion. "William, you come with me around to the front door. I shall present General Washington's letter to General Schuyler. I am sure we'll find shelter. The Schuylers are noted for their hospitality. However, we must wait to be invited."

Henry and William disappeared among the maze of outbuildings.

Jeremiah patted Rebel's neck. Then he carefully lifted her left front foot to see if a lodged stone caused her limp. The mare tossed her head and skittishly pranced on three feet.

"Shall I hold your horse while you tend her leg?" a clear high voice inquired.

Startled, Jeremiah looked up to see a slight girl watching him with bright eyes.

"I'm Nancy, Nancy Star," she volunteered. Then she gave an exasperated sigh, and added: "Now you look at me so honest like, I cannot lie to you. My name isn't Star, not really. It's Smith, but on the boat coming over here from England last spring I would look up each night and see the same star. It was as though it was watching over me. So, I said to myself, 'In my new life, in the new world, I shall call myself Nancy Star.' I'm an orphan, you see, so no one cares what name I use." She was cheerful.

Jeremiah smiled at the friendly talkative girl. "New life?" he said. "Your old one must have been very short. You don't appear to be more than twelve years old now."

"Imagine your guessing that! I tell everyone I am fourteen. Miss Betsy, that's one of the General's daughters, says I should be glad I am only twelve. And I am really, because after my five years service with the Schuylers—I'm indentured, you see—I will still be only seventeen, with plenty of time to do whatever I wish. I am not a slave, thank goodness. I wouldn't like that." She tied her blue wool shawl tightly under her chin, as though to stop her own chatter, then said, "Here now, I shall hold your horse while you look at her foot."

She held the reins and whispered softly to the mare, "There now, there now. Hold nice and still— What's her name and what is yours?" she asked as Jeremiah examined the hoof.

"Jeremiah and Rebel." She looked puzzled. "I am Jeremiah." He laughed. "No stone," he said, releasing the mare's hoof. "It must be a sprained leg."

"It should be bound then," Nancy said. "She needs rest and care. She looks tuckered out."

"Care I cannot give her," Jeremiah said. Then he told Nancy about the mission to Ticonderoga and how important it was to get the cannon to Cambridge.

She didn't seem to know much about the siege of Boston, but she listened attentively and asked an interested question now and then.

"I shall tend her for you," she said, "until you return from the north."

"You can't do that. You're only—well, only a little girl."

"You were going to say that I was only a servant," she said. Her sparkling eyes dimmed.

"Now, I didn't mean—" Jeremiah stuttered. "Why, I am a servant myself, an apprentice, the bookseller's sweeper boy, some call me. And I am an orphan too."

"But I don't mind being a servant. You sound as if you do, a little," she said. "I am learning all the time. I can bake and sew. I can even read and write some. The Schuylers are kind, and they'll let me tend Rebel. They have so many horses, one more won't matter."

Jeremiah hesitated, then protested, "I couldn't pay you for your trouble and I do like to pay my own way."

Nancy pulled her blue shawl tighter and said thoughtfully: "I understand. Well, now, being a bookseller's apprentice, maybe you would have a book in that little trunk behind your saddle. That would be good pay to me. I never had a book of my very own, except the Bible the orphanage gave me when I left England. Somebody stole it on the ship coming over. I felt bad, but not too bad. I decided that whoever did the stealing probably needed the Good Book more than me."

Jeremiah roared with laughter.

"It's a bargain, Miss Nancy," he said. "I have three books. I shall give you one, though it may not be to your liking. It's *Robinson Crusoe*, about a man shipwrecked on an island."

"Oh, I shall like that. Miss Betsy will help me with the hard words." Nancy's eyes danced and a blonde curl escaped from beneath her shawl as she nodded her head eagerly.

Now, thought Jeremiah, if he found time to read he would have to choose between *Sermons for Young Men* and his Latin grammar. It was a bleak prospect, but Nancy's delight made it seem worth while. Besides, he wouldn't lose Rebel and she would be taken care of.

After he handed Nancy the book, they gravely shook hands to seal the bargain.

The tired mare was led toward one of the barns by her new-found friend just as Henry and William returned.

As Henry had hoped, the Schuylers made the three travelers welcome. Straw pallets were spread out in a spare upstairs room in the mansion. The servants soon had a fire blazing and a substantial meal spread before them.

Later in the evening Henry went downstairs to the General's study.

"Henry just never gets tired." William groaned as he stretched out on his pallet.

Jeremiah tiptoed to the window. Beyond was the Hudson River. Only the stars brightened the blackness of the December night. They made him think of Nancy. He could see how a lonely little girl would find comfort in a twinkling star. Lonely? No, he thought, she wasn't lonely, and she didn't mind being a servant. "I am learning all the time," she had said. That was a good way to look at things. He yawned and lay down on the pallet next to the sleeping William. The next thing he knew the Sunday church bells were ringing and Henry was cheerfully humming a tune as he buttoned his vest.

"Get up, boys," said the tireless young Colonel Knox. "Your breakfast is here. The horses are ready. It's Saratoga by nightfall, and then on to Fort George. Get up, now."

They reached Fort George on Monday afternoon. The fort was crowded with Americans returning from Canada and their British prisoners of war.

Henry, William, and Jeremiah considered it a stroke of good luck to find an empty log hut in which to camp for the night. Since it was early afternoon they had ample time to gather firewood, water and feed their horses, and make themselves reasonably comfortable. Behind the hut Jeremiah found some straw. The hut's overhang had protected it from the light snow of the day before. It was clean and dry. He spread it over the dirt floor of the hut and stacked their saddlebags in one corner.

Henry came hurrying back with the disheartening information that they would have to share their quarters with a British prisoner, a lieutenant of the Seventh Royal Fusiliers who had been captured at St. Johns by Montgomery. He was being sent to prison camp in Pennsylvania where, of course, he hoped to be exchanged for some American soldier held prisoner by the British.

"William! Jeremiah!" Henry reprimanded his scowling companions. "There are many prisoners here at the fort. They must receive shelter and food. This young man seems very polite. I trust you will be gracious. He is in an unfortunate position, one in which either of you might find yourself some day."

Henry was more than polite to the young British lieutenant. He was obviously charmed by his company.

At dawn, after the lieutenant and Henry had left the cabin, William grumpily said to Jeremiah as they rebuilt the fire for their morning meal, "They talked all night and kept me awake."

Jeremiah agreed. "I didn't sleep much either. They covered everything—poetry, artillery, philosophy. Then they began talking French! Ssh! Here they come!"

Henry ducked his head as he entered the hut, a precaution his smaller companion did not have to take.

"Still talking," muttered William in Jeremiah's ear.

"Boys," Henry boomed cheerfully, "the lieutenant and I have managed to get half a loaf of bread and some honey. With the gruel, we should have a sumptuous breakfast."

The British officer sat on the straw next to Jeremiah. "Colonel Knox tells me you are quite a Latin student," he said pleasantly.

Jeremiah laughed. "Henry, the Colonel, exaggerates."

The Lieutenant did seem very nice, he thought. He had clear skin and friendly eyes. He carefully cut off less than his share of the dark bread. While Jeremiah was noticing how long and slender his hands were, the Lieutenant winced and folded his fingers over his thumb.

"A festered nail," he said apologetically in answer to Jeremiah's questioning glance.

"That can poison your blood," said Jeremiah. "That's what Dr. Warren used to say."

"I'll heat some water," William offered.

Henry's ruddy face glowed, as though "his boys" pleased him by their concern for the pleasant prisoner of war.

While Henry and William packed up in preparation for the early morning push to Ticonderoga, Jeremiah bathed the Lieutenant's festered thumb. With a clean bone needle, which they used for mending their saddle straps, he pierced the angry-looking flesh and drained it clean. Then he bathed it again and bandaged it with a strip of linen.

The Lieutenant was pleased by such "courteous attention," as he called it. "Dr. Jeremiah," he said, puckering his friendly face into a wry grimace, "would I could pay you for your services, but I cannot."

He pulled out the lining of one pocket, as though to prove his poverty. Then he said, holding up one slender finger, "Wait. I have something!"

From his other pocket he took a flat wooden box about four inches square and flipped it open, revealing an exquisitely engraved sundial. "It's very old," he said. He snapped the pocket sundial shut, smiled and bowed as he handed it to Jeremiah. "For services rendered."

"But, sir—" Jeremiah stuttered.

"I insist," said the British prisoner of war, pressing the flat box into Jeremiah's hand, "and thank you for your kindness. Perhaps, we shall someday meet under peaceful and happier circumstances. The Colonel is calling you. Good-by."

"Good-by, sir." Jeremiah suddenly remembered he did not know the Lieutenant's name.

He ran out of the cabin, not sure whether he felt sad or happy. After carefully putting his new possession in his deepest pocket, he walked toward the shore behind the Knox brothers.

William looked back over his shoulder. "Is your patient's thumb tended to, Doctor Jeremy?" he asked in a teasing tone.

Henry turned and said: "I was proud of the consideration both you boys showed the prisoner. His company to me was most enjoyable. I must remember to tell Lucy of the pleasant conversation I had with Lieutenant John André. A nice chap, a very nice chap."

So that was his name, mused Jeremiah, John André. He would try to remember. Perhaps, as the young man had said, they would meet again under happier circumstances. The war couldn't last forever.

"Come on, Jeremy," William called. "Stop dreaming!"

Jeremiah grinned. "Who's dreaming?" he shouted. "On to Ticonderoga!"

Chapter 11

As HE TOLD William after they had settled themselves in one of the fort's barrack cabins, Jeremiah did not know what he had expected of Ticonderoga, but certainly more than this. The famed Fort Ticonderoga, was a bleak structure of stone and wood with cold, ill-clad soldiers straggling about inside its embankments.

"I know," teased William, "you half expected to see Ticonderoga's ghosts of yesteryear wandering about. If it's chilled blood you want, just wait until the men seat themselves about the fire at night. It is then, I'm told, the ghosts walk, even talk out loud and tap you on the shoulder. Just wait!"

Jeremiah laughed and pretended to shake with fear. "Wait? I can't," he said.

After a day of stripping the battlements for what cheerful Henry called a "noble train of artillery" for General Washington in Cambridge, the men were weary.

When, upon his arrival, Henry had calmly announced that he planned to transport forty-three cannon all the way to Massachusetts, the men had stared at him open-mouthed. It couldn't be done! Many hinted that the jovial Colonel must be addled in the head. But Henry had laughed with his customary good nature and stated his needs—yards of three-inch rope, sturdy barges and scows to float the cannon to Fort George, and from there he planned to use sleighs and oxen or horses which he would hire from farmers who lived near by.

Now the first of the barges were repaired and loaded. More were being built. Even Henry was willing to call it a good day's work. He had retired to his bunk.

Jeremiah and William had decided to stretch their aching muscles by walking a while on the parade grounds. The sharp night air held the threat of snow.

"Henry hopes for snow after we get the cannon onto the sleighs at Fort George. He hopes the Hudson will be frozen then too," William said.

"He seems never to doubt that we'll get the cannon through."

"Henry firmly believes in a guiding ever-watchful Providence," William explained as they walked past the fort's great iron-studded door. "Henry—"

A hoarse whisper from outside the small gate inset within the huge door interrupted them. They peered through the gate. A sentry stood silhouetted there. He dropped his musket between his knees, clapped his mittened hands together, and said very low, "Be good lads and get me a hot drink from the men in that end shack there. Tell 'em Patriot Campbell is near froze."

They ran quickly to get the drink, though Jeremiah said cautiously, "A sentry isn't supposed to talk or drink while on duty. He's just supposed to watch, isn't he?"

"An icicle sentry wouldn't see much and this one is near froze. You heard him." William chuckled.

When they returned with the drink, Patriot Campbell gratefully drained the tin cup.

"Ah," he smacked his lips, "just what I needed. On such a night as this, so black, so still, Ticonderoga's past seems to come alive. It chills my bones."

He threw the cup through the gate and Jeremiah deftly caught it.

"As I stand here," continued the sentry, "I remember that the Iroquois Indians, especially the Mohawk tribe, have claimed these lakes for hundreds of years, and I get to doubting that General Schuyler, for all his skillful talk, will be able to keep them neutral in this fight. I get to re- membering, too, why the Mohawks hate the French so, why they even killed the gentle French priests who did them no harm. It was because of Samuel Champlain's unpro- voked attack on them. And now one of our own scouts, just two months ago, committed the same folly. He paid for it. They killed him. But the colonies may have to pay with many more lives. The Six Nations of the Iroquois are power- ful. Brrr! When I'm here alone I get to thinking—"

"And seeing things," said a brusque manly voice. "You Scots! Next you'll be telling that spooky tale about one of your kin, your clansman Duncan Campbell. Don't believe a word he says," said the relieving sentry merrily, as he opened the gate and took the post which Patriot Campbell eagerly left.

"What about your clansman?" Jeremiah asked, trailing after Patriot Campbell as he hurried toward the shack.

"Jeremy!" said William. "We have a full day's work ahead of us tomorrow. Come, let's go to our bunks."

"Please—" Jeremiah begged.

"You can stay, it's all right, but I'm turning in," William said as he left.

Jeremiah resolutely followed Campbell into the end shack. There were three drowsy men seated around the fire drinking from tin cups.

"So you want to hear my story?" Campbell asked Jeremiah.

The three men groaned in mock despair.

"Here's to Major Duncan Campbell of the Black Watch," said one, raising his cup. "His descendant is again about to call him forth from the grave."

Jeremiah sat cross-legged before the fire. A pleasant shiver ran up and down his back. He looked up at Patriot Campbell who turned out to be no older than Henry, about twenty-five years of age. He had dark brooding eyes and a high forehead, which wrinkled now as he put his fingers to his lips and looked around.

"It's true, every word," he said. "My grandfather, who was second cousin to Duncan himself, told my father and he, in turn, told me."

The three men hooted with laughter.

"Tell it!" said one.

"He will!" shouted another.

"Try to stop him!" declared the third.

"Well," said Patriot Campbell, seating himself on a stool, his elbows on his knees, his dark eyes peering into the fire, "years ago at Inverawe, in the Scottish Highlands, Duncan Campbell, then a trusting young man, unknowingly sheltered the murderer of his cousin Donald. This distressed Donald's ghost, of course—"

"Of course!" said one of the men, laughing. "And he tried to tell Duncan."

"Yes, he did," said Campbell, a little annoyed. "His ghost appeared again and again. But Duncan paid no heed. Finally the ghost appeared for a final visit. He bade Duncan good-by. 'Farewell,' he said gloomily, 'until we meet at Ticonderoga!' What he was saying, in fact, was that Duncan would himself die and become a ghost at Ticonderoga! To young Scottish Duncan Campbell the Indian word, Ticonderoga, meant nothing. He had never heard it before. But because of its strangeness, he remembered it."

"He didn't think seeing a ghost strange," chided one of the men, "only the word, Ticonderoga!"

"Please, let him finish," begged Jeremiah.

"Thanks, lad," said Patriot Campbell. "Well now, years later, in 1758, the British were fighting to capture this very fort from the French. The French, by the way, called it Fort Carillon, as they had a right to. They built it. Duncan Campbell had by then become a major in the Forty-second Highlanders, the Black Watch. Picture if you will, lad, my brave ancestor now in middle years, but fit and strong. His blue bonnet is slanted jauntily over one eye, his plaid kilt is flapping against his sturdy legs, and his leather pouch is swinging from the front of his belt. They are to sail north on Lake George and capture Fort Carillon, he has been told. He is eager for battle. Then, he learns the other name, the Indian name for that fort—Ticonderoga!" Patriot Campbell paused and fixed his brooding eyes on Jeremiah.

The fire had died down. The three men had crawled off to their bunks. Only their light breathing broke the silence in the shack. Jeremiah glanced around uneasily and drew his coat collar tighter about his neck. He shivered. What was it William had said? "The ghosts walk and talk, they even—" A finger tapped him on the shoulder! He jumped to his feet! Then he laughed and dropped to the floor again. It was the live Campbell, not the poor haunted one of long ago.

"Can you imagine his feelings, lad?" asked Campbell, tapping Jeremiah's shoulder again. "Did it stop him? It did not! He joined in the assault, doomed as he knew himself to be. Again and again he, with his fellow Highlanders, attacked this fort. I wish I could say they captured it. They didn't. But there is glory too in a battle well fought and lost. As you have already guessed—I can see it in your face, lad—Major Duncan Campbell was mortally wounded in that battle. But do you know, that stubborn Scot, as though to spite the ghost's prophecy that he would die at Ticonderoga, hung on to life until he reached Fort Edward. It was there he died, and it is there his body lies buried."

That night, to his surprise, Jeremiah slept exceptionally well He awoke in time to see the icy height of Sugar Loaf Mountain reflect the dawn. It glittered, changing color as the sun rose.

Henry joined him as he watched. He agreed it was a beautiful sight, but he said, "We have work to do."

Henry saw to it that the work was done. By December 9 he decided to leave William in charge of starting the barges while he rowed down to Fort George and arranged for the next lap of the journey by sleigh.

"Jeremy, you will go with me," Henry said. "We will need a messenger to keep in touch with each other. It will be a long, long noble train of artillery," he added with satisfaction.

"Are you and Jeremy leaving tonight?" William asked his brother. "It's eleven o'clock."

"The sooner the better," Henry declared.

After four hours of taking turns at rowing against ice flows, even the tireless Henry was willing to stop and rest.

Jeremiah pulled at the oars. His palms were blistered in spite of his heavy mittens. Knifelike pains kept shooting up between his shoulder blades.

"I see a campfire ahead," said Henry. "Row in toward shore."

"Yes, Colonel," he panted. "Glad to."

As he pulled on his right oar to guide the boat inland he too saw the campfire. There were several figures huddled around it. A detachment of Americans, no doubt, with more prisoners from Canada, he thought.

With his back to the shore he began to tug at both oars. Then all at once he felt the boat being pulled from behind. Its bottom scraped along the icy ground as it left the water. As he looked up, he saw Henry was staring. His usual happy serenity had vanished. He looked solemn, even a little frightened.

For one breathless moment Patriot Campbell's shivery ghost story flashed through Jeremiah's mind. Silly, he told himself, ghosts, if there are such things, don't pull boats!

Taking a deep breath Jeremiah turned around. There, looming in the darkness, stood not a ghost but a tall, fur-robed Indian, very much alive!

Chapter 12

BEING BY nature optimistic, Henry regained his composure quickly and jumped from the boat. He extended his hand toward the Indian. The red man did not seem so tall now that Colonel Knox stood next to him, but he looked just as forbidding. He kept his hands tucked beneath his fur robe.

Undaunted, Henry bowed and said: "Colonel Knox of the Continental Army. We are on our way to Fort George— er—then to General Schuyler's." When the Indian remained motionless, he added, "You know General Schuyler in Albany, sir?"

Jeremiah, still seated in the boat, began remembering all he had heard about the powerful Iroquois Six Nations. He wished Henry hadn't jumped to shore so fast. Now they could not get away if they wanted to. His rifle butt lay against his thigh. Henry's musket lay in the bottom of the boat. Jeremiah discarded the thought of using them even as it crossed his mind. Indians, he had heard, were usually friendly until attacked. He tried hard to convince himself this was true. But his hands would not relax their grip on the oars. His scalp would not stop tingling.

It was hard to see much in the dark, but just as he peered

cautiously over his shoulder at the Indian the campfire flared, as though a dry pine knot had caught fire, and Jeremiah could see the red man's face. It was not streaked with war paint. The Indian looked young, not much older than William. Jeremiah began to relax and, pulling in the oars, swung around on the seat so that he faced the shore.

Then one long coppery arm shot out from beneath the fur robe. Jeremiah sat rigid. The back of his neck prickled as he saw the Indian pointing directly at him!

"Oh," Henry explained hurriedly, "my assistant, Jeremiah Cutler."

"Maybe he doesn't understand me," Henry said as the Indian still gave no sign of his intentions.

The Indian bowed. "I understand very well," he said in a clear deep voice. "Reverend Kirkland has lived among my people for many years. We Oneidas know your language. Welcome, Colonel Knox, to you and your assistant. I am Doah-darie-yagey, grandson of Shenandoah. Come, eat by the fire, good deer meat."

"Jeremiah," whispered Henry as the Indian strode off toward the fire, "Shenandoah is an Oneida Chief. We must not offend his grandson. Indians are very touchy, I hear, very touchy. But look," he said with a shudder, "they're all dipping their hands into the same kettle."

Jeremiah jumped to shore. As he and Henry drew closer to the Indian camp a delicious smell reached them.

"I don't care how many fingers dip into that kettle, Colonel. It smells good. I'm hungry!"

The seated Indians—there were four of them—looked up and nodded when they approached. Doah-darie-yagey spread a bearskin before the fire and motioned for them to sit down and take some meat.

"Venison," said Colonel Knox.

Jeremiah bit into the meat hungrily. It had a strong taste, but it was juicy and tender. And it wasn't salted. How tired he was of salted food!

Their host squatted beside them. He would take a bite and chew, then stand erect and look around. Three times during the meal he crept toward the shore, his moccasined feet gliding soundlessly through the light snow. Each time he stood for a few minutes near the water's edge and then returned.

Jeremiah saw that beneath the fur robe the red man wore deerskin leggings and a long loose deerskin shirt fringed at the bottom, very much like his own militia shirt of homespun. And the slender Indian wore his black hair short. It hung a little below his ears. Jeremiah wondered why his head was not shaved high on either side with a stiff tuft of hair running from his forehead to the back of his neck. He had heard the Iroquois cut their hair in that fashion. During one of the Indian's trips to the lake shore, he mentioned this to Henry.

"The Mohawk warriors wear their hair that way," Henry said. "I guess each tribe of the Six Nations has different customs, just as each of our colonies has."

After they had finished the last bit of meat in the kettle and the other Indians had crawled beneath a pine-bough lean-to and gone to sleep, Doah-darie-yagey seated himself closer to Henry and said very low, "Colonel Knox, it is dangerous for you to be in Mohawk country alone."

"Dangerous? General Schuyler has had assurance from the Six Nations. They gave him their word to remain neutral at the Council Fire last August."

"That is true," agreed the Indian, "but only we Oneidas and the Tuscaroras will keep our promise, not the others, not the strongest tribe of all, the Mohawks! Colonel Johnson also held a Council two moons ago. He bade the Six Nations take up the hatchet for the King across the water. He read a letter from the King. He offered many gifts."

"They have agreed to fight against us?" Henry asked with astonishment.

"The Mohawks agreed first, then three more tribes followed. The Mohawks want the Oneidas and Tuscaroras to take up the hatchet for the King too." He nodded toward his sleeping companions and said: "We have been hunting up north. We met some Mohawks where the long lake flows into the river. They showed us their gifts. They told us that one of your scouts had attacked them last summer. It may be so. Always there is one man who will not keep the peace. But we Oneidas do not break our word because one white man breaks his. And we do not sell our word for gifts! The Mohawks and their love of gifts!" His lean jaw muscles tightened into hard knots. "The Mohawks were angry that we would not agree to join them when word comes from the King's men that the time has come to strike at your people. They are more angry right now at my hunting party than at your colonies. They do not wish us to reach Oneida territory and talk to our people. They hope to anger our tribe with lies. We will tell the truth. They will try to stop us, but we move swiftly."

So that is why the young Oneida Indian had crept so silently down to the shore and listened, thought Jeremiah. A Mohawk war party!

"It is unbelievable," muttered Henry. "Oh, I do not doubt your word, sir," he added hastily as the Oneida's nostrils flared. "I meant it is hard to imagine the Six Nations split because of our differences with the King. It is terrifying to think what this will mean to our people who live in Mohawk country if matters aren't soon settled peacefully."

"It is so," said Doah-darie-yagey. "You and the boy sleep now. I will watch. We must all rise before dawn and leave this place."

Jeremiah loaded his rifle and Henry's musket. He would sit and watch too.

After Henry had curled up by the fire, Jeremiah remained stiffly alert, his rifle between his knees.

After a few minutes he sensed the Indian watching him. He turned his head to find the lean coppery face crinkled into a smile. He had never heard of an Indian smiling! He smiled back.

"Do you not trust the sharp eyes of Shenandoah's grandson?" asked the Oneida.

"Yes. Oh, yes, I do but—" who could sleep with a Mohawk war party near by, no matter how sharp the eyes that watched?

The Indian's smile vanished. "Sleep then!" he commanded.

Jeremiah decided he would pretend to sleep, so he lay on his side still holding his loaded rifle. He tried hard to stay awake but Henry's carefree snoring soon made him drowsy. Stubbornly he lifted his sleepy head. Then the watchful Indian looked so reliable that he decided to move closer to the fire and catch just a few winks.

The next thing he knew someone was prodding him. The Oneidas had covered all traces of their camp and left before dawn, Henry told him.

"Come, boy, it's six o'clock." The Colonel was gathering their belongings. "Let's get to Fort George by noon if we can. This talk of Indian warfare disturbs me. Nothing must stop that artillery from getting through, and nothing will, so long as there's a breath left in me!"

By twelve-thirty they were at Fort George and settled in the same hut they had shared with the prisoner of war, Lieutenant André, less than a week before. Now there were only a few prisoners left in the fort, and young André was not among them.

Shortly after their arrival, three soldiers volunteered to go to Stillwater to arrange with Squire Palmer for the hiring of sleighs, yoked oxen and horse teams, and drivers. The Colonel was authorized to pay twelve shillings a day for each span of horses, and the drivers must promise to transport the cannon as far as Springfield, Massachusetts.

On the twelfth of December Henry became uneasy about William's progress with the barges, and about William himself, though he would not admit it. Jeremiah offered to row back up north again, but Henry decided to send someone else. Jeremiah, he explained, knew the way to Albany and he would need a messenger to keep in touch with General Schuyler.

Three days later, on the fifteenth of December Jeremiah left the fort on horseback with Henry's letter to General Schuyler in his saddlebag and his long rifle barrel under his knee. He was to lodge at McNeal's in Saratoga that night, rise early the next day and reach Albany by late afternoon.

It was cold and there was some snow on the ground, but it proved no hindrance. Jeremiah rode swiftly and surely without mishap. A little after four o'clock on the afternoon of the seventeenth he was riding south along Bethlehem Road toward the Schuyler Mansion. As he spied the white roof railing of the mansion in the distance, he thought longingly of a good night's rest in the pleasant upstairs guest room and remembered hungrily the good food the Schuylers served.

Leaving his horse near a barn behind the big house, he walked around to the front door and knocked. A servant opened the door promptly. Jeremiah gave him Henry's letter to General Schuyler. As he had expected, he was ushered into the spacious hall and told to wait.

In minutes General Schuyler dashed from his study at the far end of the hall. He looked very agitated as he walked toward Jeremiah waving Henry's letter.

"This will never do," he said sternly. "I have already sent out my wagon master. He is acquiring all the sleds and oxen Colonel Knox will need. Some are already on their way to Fort George."

Without further explanation the General about-faced and hurried back into his study. In a short time he emerged again, this time holding a sealed letter in his hand.

"Squire Palmer must be told immediately that his services are not needed. He will be offended, I am sure. It cannot be helped. The sooner Colonel Knox gets word to him the less inconvenienced the Squire will be."

The Albany Patroon's brown eyes snapped with decision. "You must get this countermanding order to Colonel Knox as quickly as possible. Be ready to leave early tomorrow."

The General turned on his heel and walked down the hall. At his study door he paused and said briskly, "My servant will see to your lodging, boy."

The servant puffed out his chest importantly. He asked Jeremiah his rank. When Jeremiah admitted he had none, the servant smirked as though he had known it all the time. Then he escorted the boy, not to the upstairs guest room, but out the back door to the end of the long white building behind the mansion.

Whether General Schuyler had ordered this arrangement Jeremiah had no way of knowing. Probably not. The General was a busy man. He left such details to his staff, such details, the thought came in a flare of angry humiliation, as lodgings for sweeper boys!

Hurt resentment flooded over him as the servant pointed out the men's wing of the servants' quarters. Someday, he vowed fiercely, he would become an officer in the Continental Army, someday soon. When he got back to Massachusetts he would drill and become such an expert marksman that a dozen generals would clamor to have him. He would demand a commission as a lieutenant, maybe a captain, he would—

"You've come back. How nice, Jeremiah," a gentle voice interrupted his seething thoughts.

It was Nancy Star. She stood a few yards away near one of the barns.

"I have just been feeding Rebel," she said, walking toward him. "Oh," she added, "are they making you stay out here this time?"

Jeremiah was so mad he could not speak.

"Oh, they are," she said softly as she moved closer. "And you are angry about it, too. Don't be. Come, see Rebel. She's much better, but she isn't ready for another journey I'm afraid. She won't be until spring."

Jeremiah remained standing stiffly beside the servants' quarters.

Nancy took his hand. "Oh, come now, Jeremiah. Come and pat your horse. After that I shall get you some hot water and some beef soup. Oh, what a face! Be careful, it will freeze that way."

In spite of his anger, Jeremiah smiled and allowed himself to be pulled toward the barn. Of course, he wanted to see his horse again. He was anxious to find out for himself how her sprained leg was getting along.

"That's better," Nancy said brightly. "Now forget your anger. You will sleep as well in the servants' quarters as anywhere."

Maybe he would sleep as well, thought Jeremiah, but he wouldn't forget his anger, and he wouldn't let himself forget his vow to become an officer in the Continental Army. Nothing would stop him.

Chapter 13

IN SPITE OF a hot bath and nourishing food, in spite of Rebel's whinny of recognition and a good night's rest, a trace of Jeremiah's resentment still lingered the next morning. It followed him all the way back to Fort George.

The letter from General Schuyler gave Henry great concern. How he hated to hurt anyone's feelings! Squire Palmer's answer to Henry about General Schuyler's countermanding order, which Henry had quickly sent to Stillwater, left no doubt that the Squire was deeply offended.

But a letter from his brother William at North Landing on Lake George restored Henry's usual buoyancy. He showed it to Jeremiah. A barge had sunk, but the cannon had been saved and the floating train of artillery was once again headed toward Fort George. "God send us a fair wind," wrote William.

Now the first of the barges had arrived at the fort and their cannon were being mounted on the sleds which General Schuyler's wagon master had sent. They were ready to follow the river path to Albany.

"God did send a fair wind," said Henry. "Look, Jeremiah, He is sending the snow we need too. You and I will ride on ahead to Albany tomorrow. Nothing should go amiss here at this end. The sleighs can safely crisscross the river below here, it's frozen solid. I am wary now of the final crossing at Albany. I have been talking to a man who was once a Roger's Ranger. He suggests cutting holes in the ice where we intend to cross, letting the water flood over and freeze again. This strengthens the ice. He gave me these." Henry handed Jeremiah two short iron bars bent and pronged at either end.

"What are they?" Jeremiah asked, testing the sharpness of the prongs with his finger.

"Ice grippers. You strap them to your feet so you don't slip. I have a pair for you. Well, now that you are rested and things are in order, let's be on our way. Take all your belongings, boy. We won't return."

While Jeremiah tightened the cinch straps on both their saddles, Henry stamped around happily in the deepening snow. "Just what we need. Just what we need!" he shouted happily. "A good, hard-packing snow!"

His enthusiasm continued even though the heavy snowstorm forced them to stop at a farmhouse and exchange their saddle horses for a horse and sleigh.

They had a satisfying meal at McNeal's in Saratoga and were eight miles below Saratoga at Ensign's house before dark, where they stayed the night.

The next morning when they awoke, the snow was coming down in blinding swirls. They knew they would have to walk through the woods; a horse would be too hard to guide. Even this prospect did not dim Henry's joy over the heaven-sent snow.

Immediately after breakfast Jeremiah followed him out the door. His saddlebags were slung over one shoulder and his small trunk was strapped to his back. His legs were wrapped in the strips of woolen cloth that the thoughtful lady of the house had provided. His muffler was pulled over his ears and tied under his chin. He clutched his rifle in both his mittened hands and bent his head against the raging snowstorm, staying as close behind Henry as possible.

They had plodded along only a few yards when Henry stopped so short Jeremiah bumped into him. The leader was beaming at him.

The Colonel's eyebrows and lashes were fringed with snowflakes and his full cheeks were as red as winter pippins. Jovially he thumped Jeremiah's bent back and shouted, "Merry Christmas! Merry Christmas! Ah, boy, you had forgotten."

Jeremiah sourly admitted that he had. "Sometimes," he decided privately, "Henry is just too cheerful."

They continued trudging through the deep snow until they came to a clearing and a farmhouse. The storm had stopped and Henry succeeded in buying two horses from the farmer.

They rode on and reached New City, nine miles above Albany, at dusk. There they spent the night at a small inn. The innkeeper was glad to sell them a sleigh.

By the next afternoon Jeremiah found himself approaching the Schuyler Mansion for the third time. As the sled runners crunched through the snow, a streak of stubbornness overtook him. He would not sleep in the guest room. General Schuyler could insist, Henry could beg, he would sleep in the servants' quarters.

"I understand," Henry said as they sat waiting in the hall. "You want to be near your horse." Then he went back to writing in his journal.

The General had walked toward Henry with outstretched hand. He did not even see Jeremiah.

Later, outside the servants' white building, Jeremiah had to smile at his own vanity. Why should anyone care where he slept? Why should Henry? The cannon must get through. That was Henry's only concern, as it should be. Why should General Schuyler care? Certainly he had weightier matters on his mind too. He began to feel a little ashamed of himself.

For the next three days, with the ice grippers strapped to his shoes, Jeremiah and several soldiers with three of the General's servants went out onto the river and cut holes in the ice. Each day he looked forward to evening. Then he could talk to Nancy, tend Rebel and rest his aching back.

Henry was pleased. The General was pleased. Everything was running on schedule. More horses, more sleighs, were hurrying to Fort George to bring down the cannon, and the ice trail across the river was being strengthened every day.

But on New Year's Eve the river ice began to melt and their plans with it.

"A cruel thaw," Henry lamented.

As Jeremiah told Nancy the next day, he never had seen the Colonel so discouraged.

"Don't look so sad, Jeremiah," she said soothingly. "Here, I brought you some New Year's cakes and some Dutch oleykoecks. It is New Year's Day, you know. Just think, a brand-new year. All sorts of wonderful things might be ahead."

"Mmm." Jeremiah munched the Dutch doughnut. "What sort of things?" he asked, to be polite.

"Oh, I don't know. Don't you ever pretend? What do you want to do later on?" she asked as they walked toward the barn. "Do you want to own your own bookstore?"

"Later, perhaps," he said. Then he told her about the coffee houses in New York. "I thought a combination coffee house and bookstore would be a good idea."

"Oh, yes!" she said enthusiastically. "And maybe I could serve the ladies and gentlemen. You would sell books to ladies too, wouldn't you?"

"Why, yes. Some of Henry's best customers are ladies, but Nancy, about your serving—"

"Oh, please. Say yes," she pleaded. "It's only pretend. Remember?"

Her small face looked so imploring that he smiled and said, "All right, you may serve the coffee. But that's a long way off in the future when I come of age."

"Oh, I know," she agreed.

"But right now I want to do something, something important."

"What?" she asked.

"I don't know. I guess I want to be somebody—" It was hard to explain and he was sorry he had spoken his thoughts aloud. He wanted to change the subject. He patted Rebel's neck. "I must leave her with you, Nancy. She would never last through the snow and ice. We have mountains to cross too. Do you mind keeping her a little longer?"

"Oh, no. I'll take good care of her and as soon as spring comes, Jeremiah, you can get her. I hope you come back soon, Jeremiah. I like to talk to you."

Most girls, he thought, girls like Lydia, would not be so frank. Nancy was different. That was probably, he decided, because she was only a child.

"I like to talk to you too, Nancy," he said, with equal candor. Though she chattered a lot, he thought, she listened too.

"Suppose I wrote you about Rebel. It might take the letter a long time to get to Boston, but there's always someone going downriver, and people are nice about carrying them." Her eyes sparkled at the thought. "Would you write to me too? I never got a letter."

"Neither have I," he admitted.

"Shall we write to each other then?" she said, clapping her mittened hands. "And if I make any mistakes, will you tell me? Oh, dear, it would take me a long time to find out what the mistakes were, maybe a year."

Jeremiah laughed. "Don't worry about the mistakes."

"I won't then," she declared, laughing too. "Promise you'll write?"

"I promise," he said. "Now I have to see whether Colonel Knox needs me."

"Will you come back tomorrow and talk some more?"

"If I can," he said as he left.

But there was no time during the next three days for talk. Jeremiah barely had time to eat and sleep. The river had begun to freeze again. There were more holes to cut in the newly frozen ice.

On January 4 the first cannon-laden sleighs arrived at Albany, ready for the crossing, only to have the "cruel thaw" come again. And on the same day, just as Henry was about to sit down to dinner, word came that one of the largest cannon had fallen through the ice at Half Moon Landing. Henry told Jeremiah to saddle their horses.

By nightfall they reached the landing, and Henry gave the men no rest until the cannon was rescued and reloaded. He hurriedly wrote to his brother, who was at the northern end of the artillery cavalcade, warning him of the treacherous spot.

"Here, Jeremiah," Henry said, "after you reach William stay with him. He may need you to get help if he runs into trouble. He should be at Fort Edward on the other side of the river by now."

The next morning Jeremiah started out in a light snowfall which soon turned to another blinding storm. He rode and rode, heading north toward Fort Edward, he thought.

After riding for about two hours he passed a giant oak with a low-hanging crooked branch. "It's shaped like an elbow," he thought as he ducked his head and rode on.

When, two hours later, he looked ahead and saw the same giant oak, the same low-hanging crooked branch, he knew he was lost.

The storm was over. The sun came out. All was cold and very still.

Jeremiah shaded his eyes against the glare of the white snow as he looked around. He would not panic, he told himself. The sun was overhead. He had only to stay in one spot and see which way it moved. He had not crossed the river so he must still be west of it. To the northeast lay Fort Edward. He would wait until the moving sun told him which way was northeast. He remembered the sundial in his vest pocket, but the tree shadows would do as well.

No living thing was about. His ears tingled as he sat astride his horse waiting. He pulled his muffler tighter and clapped his hands together just to break the unearthly silence. Clap—clap—clap—the sound reassured him. Until he stopped, when the clapping continued.

An echo! That was it, he told himself. But the clapping went on. Frightened now, he looked around quickly. Beyond the clump of trees where he waited was a snow-covered ledge. He thought he saw movement underneath the ledge. He reined in his horse and pulled at his long rifle. The leather thong that fastened the butt to his saddle would not loosen. He pulled off both mittens and picked at the knot. His fingers trembled.

Just then a weak voice called, "Ride away, Colonel Knox's boy. Ride away."

"Who are you?" Jeremiah demanded in as steady a voice

as he could manage. All the while he picked at the knotted thong.

"The Oneida who shared his campfire with you," the voice gasped. "Ride away."

Jeremiah breathed deeply of the clear cold air as his fear receded. He urged his horse toward the ledge, which was about two hundred feet away, and dismounted.

Doah-darie-yagey lay facing him. Jeremiah crawled beneath the ledge and knelt beside him.

"You are hurt." The Indian's forehead above his left eye was swollen to a mottled lump. "Where are your companions? Where is your robe?" The Indian lay shivering, covered only by his torn and bloody deerskin shirt and breeches. His feet were bare.

The Oneida closed his eyes, then whispered haltingly, "The Mohawks—the war party—I told you—they attacked us—I escaped—snow covered my tracks—but they will find me soon—ride away now." He raised himself on one elbow and stared at Jeremiah. His black eyes were glassy. "Ride away before the Mohawks come," he gasped before he dropped to his side and closed his eyes once more.

"Leave you? Like this? I can't do that. I'll get you onto my horse somehow." Jeremiah took off his long coat and covered the wounded Oneida. "You can tell me the way to—"

The young Indian opened his eyes and put his hand over Jeremiah's. "Look!" he whispered. "Why did you not go? Now it is too late."

Jeremiah, still kneeling, turned and looked over his

shoulder. There beneath the crooked oak branch were five mounted Indians. They were covered with fur from their necks to their ankles. He could see that their heads were shaved high on both sides, and he could see, too, their stiff black hair tufts bobbing as they bent their heads and studied his horse's tracks.

One wore a huge plume on top of his head. The others had long trailing turkey feathers stuck in their scalp locks at various angles.

Jeremiah opened his mouth to speak. He could not. He tried to move. He could not. He remained in his kneeling position and watched over his shoulder as slowly, deliberately, the plumed Mohawk drew closer, guiding his horse along the snowy trail of hoofprints Jeremiah's horse had just left behind.

Chapter 14

As a cat stalks a mouse the mounted Mohawk chief took his time advancing along the snowy trail. A light breeze ruffled his plume and Jeremiah could see a knife glittering in his hand.

The red man drew closer. His cheekbones and forehead were dabbed with crimson and white. War paint! Without a doubt, this was the Mohawk war party the Oneida had told about.

Jeremiah could not think logically but, unbidden, snatches of the Oneida's campfire talk came back to him. "They are more angry at us now than at your colonies," he had said. Jeremiah's wits quickened. That meant the Mohawks would probably not attack a white man until the King's officers so commanded. For the present all they wanted was revenge against the Oneidas who would not join in breaking the Council Fire pledge.

Were he alone, Jeremiah realized, he would have little to fear. But once this plumed Mohawk saw the Oneida the war cry would ring out.

He took a quick glance at Shenandoah's stricken grandson. He was almost completely covered by the coat. The

Mohawk must not know that Doah-darie-yagey lay concealed beneath that coat! As yet no definite plan came to Jeremiah. He only knew he must go to meet the Mohawk chief before he drew any nearer.

Scrambling hastily from beneath the rocky ledge, he stood as tall as he could and raised his hand. He had heard this was a gesture of friendship to Indians, and he prayerfully hoped it was true.

The Mohawk reined in his horse immediately. He seemed taken aback, though his painted face, lean and leathery, showed no emotion, neither surprise nor friendliness.

Jeremiah, leading his horse by the reins, walked toward the Mohawk. Every muscle in his body tightened as he forced himself to meet the warlike Indian. Clenching his jaws to keep up his courage, he kept walking, with one hand still raised.

The Mohawk fixed him with a beady glance. Without shifting that glance or turning his head, he raised his hand and shouted. The four other Mohawks instantly left the spot beneath the crooked oak branch and trotted up behind their chief.

The boy's pulse began to race as he found himself facing not one, but five Mohawks in full war paint. Indians were contemptuous of fear, he had heard. So mustering all his strength he scowled, nodded toward the rocky ledge, and said in as deep a voice as he could, "We are hunting deer."

The plumed chief remained silent.

"We are friends," Jeremiah said loudly.

One of the braves leaned over his horse's neck and mumbled in his chief's ear. The chief then looked straight at Jeremiah and said, "Two are hunting deer with one horse? Bring friend forward," he demanded, pointing toward the ledge.

Jeremiah tried to appear calm. Scowling again, he said, "My friend's horse fell. We had to shoot the horse and my friend was hurt in the fall. We will rest a while and then go home on one horse."

The Mohawk chief seemed satisfied. At least his expressionless face showed no anger. But then another brave leaned near his chief and muttered something.

The chief grunted, as though in agreement, and turned to Jeremiah once more. "You are friend to Mohawks?" he asked.

"Yes, I am a friend."

Now what shall I do, Jeremiah thought. What shall I say? For the Mohawks gave no sign of leaving. Their horses stamped in the deep snow. As they pulled on the reins to quiet their mounts Jeremiah could see their wide metal armbands reflect the afternoon's slanting sunrays. He knew now in which direction Fort Edward lay, straight ahead. But would he ever get there?

Again, unbidden, came snatches of the Oneida's talk about the campfire. "The Mohawks and their love of gifts!" Gifts, he thought. That's what they are waiting for. You were not a friend unless you gave them a gift.

He had the few shillings Henry had given him in case he needed food before he reached Fort Edward. He pulled

"A gift for the Mohawk chief."

the coins from his pocket. There were five. "What luck," he thought. "One for each of the warriors." He bowed gravely and, reaching up, offered the chief his gift.

The plumed Mohawk grunted, took the coins, turned and dropped a coin in each of his braves' open palms. Then he looked down at Jeremiah and grunted again. He held his coin up between two fingers and examined it, then he said, "One small coin for a Mohawk chief?"

He wanted more. The bandit! But Jeremiah was in no position to argue. The Indians could take everything if they chose, including his life. If they found he harbored an Oneida, they would.

"My horse for you," he said, handing up the reins.

The painted chief brushed the reins aside. "Have horse," he said.

Jeremiah hurriedly began to untie his rifle, but the chief's next words stopped him. "No gun. Have gun. Colonel Johnson gives many guns."

Desperately Jeremiah tried to think. What else did he have to offer? The sundial, the pocket sundial Lieutenant André had given him. He dug into his pocket and drew forth the square wooden box.

"A gift for the Mohawk chief," he said, holding the box up on his open palm.

The Mohawk looked at the flat wooden square with disdain. His thin lips tightened. Just then Jeremiah flipped open the box and the Mohawk's eyes brightened with childish delight. Jeremiah hurriedly pointed to the sun, then the dial, explaining the sundial's usefulness.

The Mohawk cut short his explanation. "I know. This is a good gift."

Without another word he grabbed the sundial, kicked his horse, and motioned for his braves to follow. Past the rocky ledge the war party trotted without a backward glance.

Jeremiah threw his arms about his horse's neck. After the moment of dizzy relief passed, he walked slowly back to the rocky ledge where the Oneida still lay curled beneath the coat. First of all, he thought, he must try to build a fire. Without his warm coat he was miserably cold. During the tense encounter with the Mohawks he had not noticed it, nor his increasing hunger. His whole being had been intent on staying alive. But cold could kill too.

Nature had provided a dry shelter beneath the ledge. It needed only warmth to make it safe and comfortable. The Oneida would know how to find firewood even in the snow, he thought, as he crawled beneath the ledge and gently shook the Indian.

"You did well," said the Indian. "You saved my life."

Weak as he was, he managed to give Jeremiah instructions about building the fire. He told him to gather bark from the pine and cedar trees and then crumble the dry inner layer, into a pile and light it with his flint. Once this blazed, he said, even damp twigs and branches would burn.

Soon their rocky shelter grew warm. Jeremiah tied his horse near the fire. He tried to plan his next step. In spite of a grinding hunger, which he knew both the Indian and his horse shared, he decided they must stay where they were until morning. There was no longer enough daylight left for a journey to Fort Edward. The sun told him that. Then, after a night's rest his Indian companion might be stronger.

All through the cold night he kept the fire burning, but as the sun rose he let it die.

Jeremiah mounted first, then the Oneida painfully pulled himself up behind the saddle and grasped Jeremiah about the waist. Doah-darie-yagey now wore the long coat for disguise as well as warmth. Jeremiah had insisted on the precaution.

They jogged along slowly for two hours without seeing a rabbit, a bird, or a sign of human life. But finally, a little way ahead, they saw a curl of smoke rising above a clump of pine trees.

Jeremiah dismounted and looked around. It would be wisest to investigate first. He took his rifle and stepped through the deep snow toward the trees. Moving silently from one snow-laden pine tree to another, he soon saw the campfire. He moved closer. One lone white man sat hunched before the fire. A hunter, Jeremiah thought, feeling safe. He called and boldly stepped out into the open.

In a flash the hunched figure jumped up and hoisted a long slender gun to his shoulder. Jeremiah reacted instantly. He raised his own rifle.

"Wait!" shouted the hunter. "Don't shoot! I know ya could hit me. I taught ya myself."

Jeremiah looked again. This gaunt bearded face with its

sunken eyes was not familiar to him. Then the eyes blinked
and the hunter laughed, a familiar growling laugh.

"Thompson!" Jeremiah shouted. "Mr. Thompson!"

He ran toward the Virginia rifleman crying, "Mr. Thompson, what are you, how did you—?"

Chapter 15

RIFLEMAN THOMPSON soon had his unexpected guests warmed and fed. He had gotten provisions from Fort George. They were nearer to Saratoga than Fort Edward, he told Jeremiah. If it was the artillery train he was looking for he had better start out fresh the next morning and hightail it back to Albany, because the last of the loaded sleds had already left Saratoga. He had seen them.

"I come as far as the Richelieu River with Sergeant Antil," he explained, after they had gathered firewood for the night and made a lean-to of pine boughs.

"Who is Sergeant Antil?" Jeremiah asked, though he was thinking how good it felt to have his coat back. Doahdarie-yagey was wrapped in Thompson's blanket. And he was wondering if ever salt pork would taste so good again.

"Sergeant Antil is one of Arnold's men. He's goin' to Montreal to get help. They can't give him any more men. Wouldn't do no good anyhow."

"What happened?" asked Jeremiah, alert once more.

"What happened?" Thompson snorted, rubbing his wiry beard with the back of his hand. "Everything! Since we left Cambridge last September, everything! We pushed

through them woods to Canada. Took us weeks, months.
Half the men died. Us that was left was stewing our leather
pouches and belts for food 'fore we reached Quebec. And
the cold! Then Montgomery got there. It all began to seem
worth while. There was great plans afoot to take Quebec.
We was ridin' high. Montreal was won, and St. Johns.
Quebec was next."

Thompson stood up and began to pace before the fire.
"Montgomery planned to attack from Cape Diamond on
the south," he continued. "Arnold and Morgan from St.
Roche on the north. It was all set. Then a terrible blizzard
come up—hail, snow, wind. We couldn't see. Our fingers
was numb. But the attack got under way. We were making
headway. Got past the town's first barricade. Even got
a welcome from the French folks. *Vive la liberté!* they
shouted at us. Then Arnold was hit. His leg was bleeding
bad. They dragged him to the rear lines and Morgan took
over. We got deeper into town and headed toward the
center, watching all the time for Montgomery to come
from the south. We rounded up a lot of prisoners. That's
what we thought, anyway. Then we was trapped, just
trapped."

Rifleman Thompson sat beside Jeremiah and hunched
his shoulders as though remembrance made him shudder.
"Montgomery was dead. They told us he died in Aaron
Burr's arms. I got away, back to Arnold. He's not giving
up, he says. Get men, he says. We need more men, he
shouts. He sent Sergeant Antil to Montreal. He was
headed that way when I left him."

The rifleman pulled at his gaunt face. "Don't think I'm giving up, boy. But seeing Morgan taken—he cried like a baby he did—well, it's all just knocked the wind outa me. I'm going home. My time is up anyway. I'll sign up again if I ever get warmed through. Wasn't them British that licked us. It was the winter."

Jeremiah remembered the men swinging out of the Cambridge camp so confidently last fall. Now half of those men were dead and the rest were trapped.

He couldn't think about it now, he told himself. He had to reach the artillery train. Maybe the Knoxes had already met. Maybe they had given him up for lost. Maybe they were wasting precious time looking for him.

The Oneida, Thompson said, could stay with him until he became stronger. "I don't take to Indians usually, but this one seems all right. I'll look out for him."

Thus assured, Jeremiah started out the next morning. From Saratoga to Albany was less than a day's journey even in the deep snow, and he reached the Schuyler Mansion in the early afternoon.

As he trotted south along Bethlehem Road, a glorious sight lay before him. There, as far as the eye could see, slipping and skidding, but moving slowly eastward across the frozen river, were the horse-drawn, cannon-laden sleighs.

He found Colonel Knox at the icy riverbank with no time to hear explanations. "So long as you are safe; there's no time to talk now. You go with William. He will lead the largest group, fourteen sleighs in all. I will stay here until the last sled crosses and then ride ahead and join you."

Jeremiah thought he should say good-by to Nancy, but there was no time. He wondered whether she would remember to write to him.

He dismounted and led his horse across the river, avoiding the gaping hole one of the drivers warned him about. One of the precious cannon had broken through the ice there and slid from sight.

A proud thrill shot through him as he stood on the eastern riverbank and watched the artillery train cross. An impossible task, so many had said.

A hand fondly touched his shoulder. It was William. "Glad you are safe." Then he too looked across the river. "A magnificent sight, Jeremy. I don't think I really believed it was possible, but Henry never doubted for a moment."

By the tenth of January they were crossing the mountains. People left their warm houses and came plodding through the snow to cheer them on.

At Springfield the New York drivers, as agreed, turned back with their sleds, horses, and oxen. Massachusetts farmers provided fresh teams and drivers for the next lap of the journey to Cambridge.

When they arrived there on January 24 the camp went wild with excitement. The men, and women too, swarmed about the sleighs. Henry gave his permission for one cannon to be fired in celebration. Then he called William and Jeremiah to him, and they all went into one of the Marbleheader's neat sail tents. There, by candlelight, Henry read aloud his accounts.

"If I have forgotten anything, tell me."

Neither of them could think of an omission. So Henry opened his journal and carefully made his last entry.

For expenditures in a journey from camp around Boston to New York, Albany and Ticonderoga—and from thence, with 55 pieces of iron and brass ordnance, one barrel of flints and 23 boxes of lead, back to camp (including expenses of self, brother, and servant) £520.15.18¾.

"By the way, Jeremy," Henry said, "I have written a report for General Washington of your conversation with the Virginia rifleman. I hoped there had been some mistake about General Montgomery's death, but several rumors around camp confirm the whole terrible defeat in Canada."

When he received no answer, Henry remarked, "You're very quiet, boy." He pointed to the journal. "You don't mind being listed in Congress' records as a servant, do you?"

"No, Henry, I don't mind. I'm tired, that's all."

"Of course you are." Henry closed the journal. "This is a great day for all of us," he said solemnly. "Do you realize that in a very short time these cannon will free our beloved Boston?"

The Knox brothers left the tent and Jeremiah stayed inside, watching the candle sputter. It was true, he thought, he didn't mind being listed as a servant. At one time he might have, even a very short time ago. But not now. Perhaps he was growing up. Growing up—could that explain, too, this feeling he had of loss and emptiness? It had come upon him when Henry had mentioned Boston. Of course he wanted Boston to be free. He wanted the Knoxes to get back their shop. He wanted to work in the bookstore again and he guessed someday he wanted a bookstore of his own. Someday—but it no longer seemed so exciting.

Once the Boston bookstore had been his whole world. During the past year his world had grown, so swiftly.

It was as though a pebble had been thrown into a pond that day last spring when he left Boston for Concord. Or had it started with Roger and the eggs? Anyway, from that time forward, like circles in the water growing larger and larger, his world had widened.

These last two months had been a wonderful adventure, at times too perilous. Once or twice, he admitted now to himself, he had wished himself safely locked up in the bookstore on Cornhill. But now with Boston sure to be freed, his old life was close at hand. It seemed too safe, too dull. Unimportant, that was the word. What did he want? Surely not danger every day of the week. No. As he had told Nancy, he wanted to do something important. Helping transport the cannon from Ticonderoga to Cambridge had been important, even though his own part in it had been small. How could he go back to being a bookseller's apprentice again?

Chapter 16

A BOOKSELLER'S apprentice? His old life? Never again, Jeremiah soon discovered. One word, like a dash of ice water across his face, made him realize that this fight to free Boston had become a war. One word—independence! And level-headed Henry, of all people, said it.

It was on Sunday evening, March 17. Colonel Knox jackknifed his huge frame as he entered the tent where Jeremiah and William sat on a low slab bench relishing some fresh fried codfish.

Henry had just come from a meeting with the selectmen of Boston, and these gentlemen had reported that the last of General Howe's soldiers had left town. General Gage had long since sailed for England, leaving General Howe in command. Now, though some British ships still lingered in the harbor, Boston was completely evacuated. "They admitted that without those guns from Ticonderoga," Henry reported proudly, "the victory might not have been so swift."

This was great news to the young codfish eaters. Jeremiah jumped to his feet and whacked his head soundly on the tent's wooden support.

He smiled and rubbed his head ruefully. "Just like that, the King will come to his senses once General Howe reaches England with news of his defeat. Our charter will be restored all right."

He noticed the Knox brothers exchanging solemn glances.

"Well, won't we have our free charter? And in a few days we shall all be back in the bookstore again. Won't we?" he persisted when William and Henry remained silent and sober faced.

Henry cleared his throat. "Jeremy, the British are not defeated. General Howe is not sailing for England. He'll send to England for more troops to be sure, but right now he's headed for Halifax. There he will plan his next move, another attack, probably against New York. Our fight for independence has just begun."

Jeremiah stifled a gasp. Independence!

"Don't you see?" William asked. "It's too late for a restored charter now."

Henry's full face grew red. "It is independence or absolute servility to the Crown forever after!"

Jeremiah had heard talk of independence before. Mr. Samuel Adams had spoken of it many times, but no one seemed to take it seriously. Now, for the first time, he realized there was no longer another path. The King had refused the colonies fair treatment for years before Lexington, Concord, and Bunker Hill, and the siege of Boston. Would he restore their rights now, after his soldiers had been killed and wounded, his forts captured, his ships cannonaded out of Boston Harbor? Not only was Massachusetts involved. All the colonies had sent men to the camps around Boston. Would the King allow any of these colonists to keep their properties? General Washington his Virginia plantation? General Schuyler his vast New York estates? Henry his bookstore in Boston? Nathanael Greene his Rhode Island iron foundry? Never! These men would lose everything, probably their very lives, and so would the men who had fought with them.

He could see it all in a new light now. A restored charter for Massachusetts was no longer possible. The thirteen colonies were now involved. Independence for all must be won.

"General Washington is sending troops to New York tomorrow," Henry continued. "Very shortly I shall follow with the artillery, together with General Greene, General Heath, and their brigades. Lucy insists she will accompany me, so it will be up to you, William, to re-establish the bookstore. Salvage what you can. Our losses must be tremendous. Finances, unfortunately, have become a real problem. I wish I could serve without pay as General Washington does. I wish I could feed and clothe my men as General Schuyler is doing. I cannot. I shall be grateful if I can support my wife, pay you boys fair wages, and have a going business waiting for me after the war. I know I can depend on you both. Jeremy, you will have to take over the printing and binding. William, get a boy to sweep and sort stock."

Jeremiah knew then that his old life was gone forever. It was good to be back in Boston again, once the shock of seeing its devastated condition had passed. The Old South Church, where Dr. Warren had spoken just the year before, had been stripped of its pews and galleries by the British. They had turned it into a graveled riding ring.

Town House and Faneuil Hall had also been damaged by the departing Redcoats. But, as William remarked, Boston could have suffered the same fate as Charlestown did during the Bunker Hill battle. It could have been left a heap of smoldering ashes.

It was good to be back in the bookstore on Cornhill again. After William sorted the scattered, dusty books, and Jeremiah repaired the broken shelves and replaced a missing door hinge, they agreed it began to look like home.

In order to save on expenses, William rented the Knox house and partitioned off the back of the store for his and Jeremiah's sleeping quarters.

It was good to be able to wash regularly again, Jeremiah thought, to keep his hair brushed and tied, his newly sprouted chin whiskers shaved, and to have the same warm dry place to sleep each night.

He had money in his pocket, too! To his surprise, his trip to Ticonderoga had earned him wages. He needed them. All his clothes were too small. Fortunately, at Brimmer's he was able to buy new breeches, two pairs of stockings, two shirts, a buff vest, and a wine-colored coat.

How satisfying it was to drill with the militia once more, the Boston militia, since he had transferred from Cambridge. His new captain praised his marksmanship and military bearing, in spite of his too-short militia shirt. Because of this praise, Jeremiah couldn't help renewing the vow he had made that dismal winter's night in Albany, this time without bitterness, to become someday an officer in the Continental Army. It was no longer a selfish dream, a wish for personal glory, though pride was involved. Now a war was being fought, for independence, and he wanted to help, to do something important again.

The militia captain told him that General Washington expected to be calling on the companies for men very soon. "On the day you are sixteen, this coming October," he told Jeremiah, "you can sign up with the army. You'll be a welcome addition with that rifle."

William, too, dreamed of a more exciting life, Jeremiah soon discovered.

It was late May, and they had been busy all day supplying eager customers with copies of Thomas Paine's pamphlet, *Common Sense.*

"Mr. Paine is an Englishman," Jeremiah remarked. "Strange he should feel as he does. We are obligated, according to him, to win this war not only for ourselves, but for people all over the world, now, and for all time to come. Whatever does he mean by that?"

"I don't exactly know," William admitted. "I only know, Jeremy, that as soon as this store and its finances are in better condition, I am joining Henry. You can keep the store as well as I. I'm tired of reading pamphlets about this war. I intend to do something about it! Henry

Jeremiah sat down at once and wrote to Nancy. Even if the post road remained open to lower New York, he knew his letter might not get upriver for months, but he felt less guilty about forgetting his promise after he had signed and sealed his answer.

He wrote his thanks for her letter and her care of Rebel. He expected to enlist soon. His bookselling would have to wait until the war ended, and so would the coffee house-bookstore they had talked about together, he added, hoping it would please her that he remembered. Would she write to him again and send it to the bookstore on Cornhill. "From there, it will be forwarded to me in camp, where-ever I may be."

Jeremiah did not join the Continental Army on his sixteenth birthday. By then William lay on his cot wracked with chills and fever. For weeks he hovered close to death.

Chapter 17

ALL THROUGH the winter and into the spring of 1777 Jeremiah kept postponing his enlistment.

As the first of each month rolled around he would think: "Before the end I will leave William. He is getting stronger. With Georgie's help he soon will be able to manage the bookstore again."

William's recovery, however, was slow.

April passed, May, June, July. Boston buzzed with news. A British raid in Connecticut, an American victory off the South Carolina coast, Washington's army in Jersey was growing, Congress had fled Philadelphia, Congress had returned, a young French nobleman, the Marquis de Lafayette, had landed and was on his way to General Washington.

News came from George Rogers Clark of the terrible sufferings of Kentucky's settlers.

It was rumored that the British planned to sweep down from Canada and up from New York city which they now held. This would cut the colonies in two.

With each bit of news Jeremiah's restlessness increased. He had informed Henry of his brother's illness. Surely, he thought, Henry would argue against William's joining him. But on the last day of July, the same day the news came that the French fleet had been sighted off Newport, a letter came from Henry and Jeremiah's plans crashed once more.

Henry, now a brigadier general, recounted the retreat to White Plains the previous fall, the abandonment of the two American forts on opposite sides of the Hudson River, the retreating race through Jersey, and finally the December victory at Trenton. "We have fought Hessians, Highlanders, Lord Percy's battalions, and at last proved our worth. We defeated the British at Princeton, and General Howe is said to have revised his low opinion of our General and our men."

Dan Morgan and his riflemen had been with the army, but expected to go north to strengthen General Schuyler's defense against the British in Canada. "Camp life is rigorous, dear brother," Henry wrote. "We are ragged and often hungry. You must not join me until your full strength returns. Perhaps next September, after God's summer sun has renewed your vigor."

William talked of nothing but his departure in September.

News came to Boston during the late summer of terrible hand-to-hand battles in the Mohawk Valley at Fort Stanwix and Oriskany, of the loss of Ticonderoga to the British, of an entire farm family being brutally scalped by Indians. Jeremiah's feeling of uselessness grew.

Meanwhile William was busily preparing to leave Boston.

The American army was between General Howe and Philadelphia, Henry had written. "It is more numerous than ever in spite of Morgan's departure to Saratoga. Come to Chester, William or thereabouts. Travel cautiously. There are bands of ruffians with loyalty to neither side, who rob, kidnap, and try to sell information to us and to the British." Henry feared the British General Cornwallis would succeed in recapturing Philadelphia. "There is no despair in camp, however, in spite of our defeat at Brandywine."

By the time this letter reached Boston, it was known that Cornwallis had taken Philadelphia, and that Congress had once more fled. This did not deter William.

Before his departure he stood for a moment beside his mount. "Jeremy, perhaps you think I should let you, who are more able-bodied, go instead. I should, I know. I won't be much use to the army after a short time. But, Jeremy, I want to go, for even that little while."

"I know how you feel, William," Jeremiah said.

"Here's something you don't know." William smiled. "I have arranged with my brother for you to take my place as a volunteer aide-de-camp in two months' time. Now do you forgive me for leaving you with all these musty books?"

As the weeks went by, Jeremiah began to plan again. News came of the American victory at Saratoga. The British invasion of northern New York had failed. Then came word that British ships were sighted in Delaware Bay —His Majesty's Navy—the very words were frightening.

From Washington's Headquarters came news of a strenuous battle at Germantown. Jeremiah's seventeenth birthday passed, and day by day he looked for William. Instead, a letter from Henry arrived at the end of October, stating that "Billy was withstanding the hardships amazingly well." Then in late November came a letter from William himself. "I would like to stay longer, but will return if this is not agreeable to you. I remember well my promise that you could take my place in two months' time."

Once more Jeremiah's plans were ruined. How could he refuse William's plea? But he was so disappointed that he put off answering immediately.

One afternoon his militia captain stepped into the book-store with a piece of astonishing news. He, Jeremiah Cutler, was being offered a lieutenant's commission under the Marquis de Lafayette. The young Frenchman had been authorized by Congress to plan an expedition into Canada. All militia captains had been ordered to recommend suitable men and Jeremiah, because of his ability and his experience in northern New York, had been chosen. He must, however, leave within ten days. He could go or not as he chose, the militia captain said, adding as he left: "I realize your predicament. However, I suggest you ask young Knox to return immediately. A lieutenant's commission is not likely to come your way again for sometime."

Over and over Jeremiah wrestled with himself. How often he had said he would do anything for the Knoxes, they had been so good to him.

All Henry had asked was that his business be kept going until after the war. "I'm counting on you both," he had said. Now all William asked was a little more time away from his responsibility, time which only Jeremiah could give.

And, Jeremiah had to admit to himself, it wasn't a choice between joining or not joining in the fight. It had become a choice between disregarding William's plea and going as Lieutenant Cutler immediately, or giving William the time he wanted and going later as plain Jeremiah, volunteer aide-de-camp.

The fantastic vow he had made to become an officer, to be somebody, might be fulfilled. How could he throw away his opportunity? Hadn't he said that nothing would stop him? But how cast aside his debt of gratitude to the Knoxes?

The more he pondered, the harder his decision became. In this frame of mind he wrote to Nancy, though as yet he had received no answer to his first letter and a full year had passed.

A terrible thought came to him as he wrote. The fighting had been fierce in northern New York. Suppose Nancy —but, no, he couldn't imagine Nancy not chattering, laughing, and looking up at the stars.

Lydia entered the bookstore just as Jeremiah sent Georgie off with the letter to find the courier. She brought news that made his decision even harder.

"Do you remember Roger?" she asked as she ran her gloved fingers over the books. "Lord Percy has sailed for England, and Roger has joined a regiment in Philadelphia. He's a Royal Fusilier Captain now, if you please. My, he's pushing his way to the top. Sam is raging, my mother says. On the very day he is sixteen he declares he will run all the way from Worcester to General Washington."

So Roger was now a captain and Jeremiah was still plain Jeremiah. He could imagine Roger saying, "Still a book-seller's sweeper boy! Indeed!"

A week passed and Jeremiah had not decided. Then a letter came from Henry full of gratitude for his respon-sible management of the bookstore, his loyalty, he called it. "There will be a grand reunion in Boston during Febru-ary. Lucy, William, you and I will be a family once more for a little while. Then you will accompany me back to camp as my aide. It will be a happy association. I am count-ing on it."

Jeremiah's decision was made, and Lieutenant Cutler became a vanished dream. He must refuse the commission, he told his militia captain.

In a very short time word came that not only had Lieu-tenant Cutler vanished, but the expedition to Canada as well. Henry's January letter from Valley Forge bristled with indignation. "A plan is being uncovered, a plot to replace General Washington. A twenty-year-old French nobleman was to be used in the first step to override our General's command. He proved wiser than I gave him credit for. This Marquis de Lafayette saw through the plan almost at once, and he let the group of schemers know where his loyalty lay, with General Washington! I regret to state that General Gates' ambition for the highest command is rumored to have started the whole sorry affair. It failed, or will, of course, but it has left deep scars of

self-doubt on our beloved Commander. He moves wearily
among our ragged men here. Those sick with smallpox he
freely tends, being himself immune. He worries over us
all, encourages us, listens to our complaints, and then goes
off by himself to pray for new strength. How can they
imagine they could replace such a man?"

It seemed incredible to Jeremiah that anyone could plot
against General Washington, putting ambition above
loyalty. Then he realized with a start that this was the very
problem he, himself, had so recently found such a struggle.

A few days after the family reunion in Boston, two
letters from Nancy came together. Jeremiah read them
aloud to the Knoxes. The more recent one confirmed
Henry's information. The first was dated:

Dear Jeremiah,   *October 30, 1777*

*Yr letter came before the terrible times we had here.
I did not have a way to answer. Four British armies
were coming to take Albany. That was last June. The
army from New York (where our coffee house will be)
never got here. The one from the Mohawk Valley was
beaten bad by our people and so were the two others.
A lot of soldiers were killed. Genral Schuyler's house
was burned up. The one upriver further, not the one
you were at here. A young lady named Jane Mc-
Crea was scalped by the Britisher Indians. We were
all scared to go out of the house after that.*

*The British took that fort you were at, Ticonderoga.
We got it back again now though.*

A deserter tried to get Yr Horse. I hit him with my broom. I screamed too. He ran away. Yr Horse is fine. Hope you are well.

Yr friend,
Nancy Star

The second letter read:

Febrary 2, 1778

Dear Jeremiah,

I got your letter. I was surprised it came from Boston. You hoped to be a lieutenant you said with the Frenchman, but thought you might have to say no. I guess you did and that was lucky. It was all wrong, the whole plan, our Genral Schuyler said, and now the Frenchman is here he says so too. It was another Genral trying to get to be head of the army instead of Genral Washington. People up here know that our Genral and Arnold planned for our men so they beat the British and made them give up at Saratoga. The Morgan men were there with their long guns too. But Genral Gates told all about himself and he got all the cheering. Now our Genral has got no army and Genral Arnold, who is in the hospital here with a bad leg, is very mad.

I hope you get to be a lieutenant if you want. Yr Horse is fine. I am growing a little. I will be fourteen in three months so I pinned up my hair.

Yr friend,
Nancy Star

P.S. The British Genral Burgoyne stayed here before he started for your Boston. He gave Miss Betsy his shoe buckles. I will show you when you come.

Another P. S. Miss Betsy and I made the new flag that Congress approved. We used her white petticoat, the Genral's old blue coat and some red flannel. It is very pretty. I am so glad it has stars.

After Jeremiah finished reading, Henry said slowly, "I didn't know you had been offered a commission and refused."

Jeremiah didn't explain why he had refused, but Henry looked as though he had already pieced together the whole story.

"Your little friend's letter is clearer than many lengthy reports I have read, Jeremy."

"At Saratoga the British gave up their reputation of being unbeatable," William commented.

Lucy whispered, "And there will be Whigs in London who will cheer our victory."

"My love," said Henry, "it is no longer Whigs against Tories. It has grown much larger. France is about to declare war against England. Spain and Holland, it is rumored, will soon follow."

"I, for one, don't like this foreign interference," declared Lucy.

"It is deplored by many," Henry agreed. "Independence once won will have to be guarded. But it is impossible not to like some of the men this foreign interference has brought us, the German, Von Steuben, and young Lafayette, for instance." He turned to Jeremiah and said cheerfully: "Lucy plans to come to Pennsylvania in May. You and I will return to camp at Valley Forge in a few weeks. You haven't changed your mind about being my aide-de-camp, have you? I can't promise you a commission, not right away, that is."

"Of course I'm going with you, General," Jeremiah said promptly. Then he grinned and added, "Try to stop me."

William chuckled. "Did you tell Jeremy who wanted the post provided a colonel's commission and £100 went with it?"

"Who?" asked Jeremiah, thinking he couldn't stand another change of plans.

"It was after news came of the victory at Saratoga," Henry said. "And if there's anyone I detest it's a traitor, a man who believes in neither our cause nor the King's, who wants only personal gain and glory on the winning side."

"There are such men on our side too, Henry," interrupted Lucy. "One I wouldn't trust is General Charles Lee. He's shifty-eyed. I met him in Cambridge."

"Lucy!" said Henry sharply.

"Well, Henry dear, which Redcoat approached you?" asked Lucy, looking not the least ashamed of her previous remark.

Henry hitched around in his chair uncomfortably. Finally he said: "I shall tell, only because it's an example of the sort of thing we must expect. But this is in confidence, you understand. I don't like disregarding even a traitor's request for secrecy." Henry lowered his voice. "It was during an exchange of prisoners, Jeremy. And it was Roger, Lord Percy's former ward, you remember, who took me aside and tried to sell his loyalty to the Crown."

Jeremiah felt his mouth drop open. Roger!

Chapter 18

IT WAS MAY 15. Jeremiah had been at Valley Forge for two months. Besides seeing again General Washington, General Greene, and General Charles Lee, glumly silent since his recent imprisonment by the British, Jeremiah had caught glimpses of the blond Frenchman, Lafayette, the dashing Anthony Wayne, Dan Morgan himself, and Ethan Allen too, who reported to General Washington after his release by the British and then returned to his beloved Vermont. Jeremiah had seen the bold Captain McLane, the celebrated General Benedict Arnold, whose leg had not completely healed, and who had been promised the command of Philadelphia, once it was recaptured. And, of course, Jeremiah had seen, and heard, the German drillmaster, Baron Von Steuben.

Because of the Baron, most of Jeremiah's time had been spent in writing. Baron Von Steuben spoke only German and French. Though he memorized the English translation of his commands, he would often forget and bark out an order in French or German. When the soldiers scattered every which way, his heavy jowls would redden, his bushy eyebrows quiver, and then he would wave his arms and shout his exasperation in a mixture of languages until every soldier, the Baron included, doubled up with laughter. Though this added to the middle-aged German's popularity, it was not efficient. Soon a system was started whereby the Baron wrote his regulations in French and his aide translated them into English. After Alexander Hamilton passed on the translation, it was copied many times by the various aides and distributed to squad leaders.

But now the "new" American army at Valley Forge was all an army should be. The dreadful winter was over. There had been a big celebration the week before, a parade, games, and refreshments served by Mrs. Washington, Mrs. Greene, and Lucy. And at last the tedious writing was over for Jeremiah.

It was a misty spring morning. Jeremiah was cleaning his rifle when Henry, who had just returned from a conference with General Washington, approached.

"News has come through the lines, Jeremy, that General Howe is returning to England leaving another in command of Philadelphia. A Major André is said to be planning a most elaborate farewell party. I wondered if it could possibly be the same André we met at Lake George two and a half years ago. But no matter. During the change-over we hope to recapture Philadelphia. Lafayette is being given a sizable force to explore the enemy lines, a New Hampshire brigade, some Pennsylvania militia men, and Captain Allen McLane's band."

"Captain McLane's raiders got food and blankets for this camp last winter, didn't they? Are they Pennsylvanians too?"

Henry smiled. "They are everything, a powerful mixture of militia men, farmers, riflemen, and often a band of Oneida Indians joins them."

"Everything?" asked Jeremiah cautiously. "Would Captain McLane take a volunteer aide-de-camp on this expedition? Please, Henry—General Knox!"

Henry laughed, but his only answer was, "We shall see." Then he pointed up the road and said: "Walk to that bend, then turn left and follow the footpath. What you see will surprise you."

Puzzled, Jeremiah obeyed. He had not walked very far along the footpath when a shout made him spin around.

"Jeremiah! Sons of Liberty together again! It's me! It's Sam!"

The two boys studied each other, grinning face to grinning face. Sam's freckles were more profuse than ever, Jeremiah saw, but his wild straw-colored hair had been tamed and tied. Though he hadn't grown tall, he was sturdy. How good it was to see him again!

"There's an expedition going out in a few days. I've been training with the Worcester militia. Do you think they might let me go?" Sam asked, after they had exchanged pieces of news.

Jeremiah laughed and repeated Henry's words, "We shall see."

That very night General Knox brought word that Lafayette would need two more scouts. Three days later Jeremiah and Sam had crossed the river and were encamped with the army at Barren Hill, two miles from the British lines outside Philadelphia.

It was at dusk on the nineteenth and they were still awaiting orders.

"From this hill you can see what a good position General Lafayette has chosen," Sam said. "See, we overlook all the main roads. He has each one covered and we can advance in several directions."

"We can also be attacked from several directions and we can't ford the river here if we have to retreat in a hurry. Think what a prize the Marquis would be now that France and England are at war!"

Sam thrust out his chin. "Why talk of retreat? Who wants to retreat?"

Jeremiah patted his friend's back. "You're right, Sam. We're not here to retreat but to get information about the enemy and advance the lines nearer Philadelphia. We'll do it!"

Just then a sergeant came to say that General Lafayette wished to see them.

The young Frenchman held a spy glass in one hand.

"Ah," he greeted them, "my scouts, ardent to reconnoitre for me! Captain McLane is to the south on Ridge Road. I would greatly value *une nouvelle*, that is, a piece of news from him. Do the British march? If so, how many? You will go, both of you, *immédiatement*, but with caution."

It didn't take them long to gather their guns and ammunition. Soon they were treading soundlessly along the soft shoulder of Ridge Road.

"I can't see," whispered Sam. "Don't go so fast."

"Hold to my shirt and be quiet," warned Jeremiah.

In this fashion they had walked about two miles when suddenly Jeremiah felt a hand clap across his face. From the muffled sound behind him he knew Sam was being treated in the same way.

"Show your paper!" came a demanding whisper.

On the pass being presented, the hand dropped from his mouth and obviously from his companion's too, for Sam protested, "Who is it, Jeremiah?"

"Shhhhhh! Shhhhhh! Shhhhhh!" The warning hisses came from all about them.

"Oneidas, Captain McLane's," whispered Jeremiah to Sam. He had recognized the deep voice as Indian. He wondered if by chance one of these red men would know Doah-darie-yagey, but when he started to question the Oneida at his side he was given a warning poke in the ribs.

A thunderous sound of galloping horses drew near. The Indians, Jeremiah realized, had heard it long before.

"Dragoons!" whispered the Oneida to Jeremiah. "Stay here, you and boy. Watch!"

As the galloping British cavalrymen drew near, the air filled with bloodcurdling Indian war whoops and ear-piercing shrieks. The horses reared, pivoting on their hind legs. Swords rattled as the dragoons tried to control their terrified mounts. Some could do nothing but let them streak back down the road. Others struggled, but without success. Finally the last dragoon gave up and galloped off.

"Now, we talk," said the Indian. "Captain McLane is on way to camp to tell British are coming fast on three roads. You and boy go back."

Jeremiah and Sam started back. After they had traveled in silence for a mile or so Jeremiah whispered, "Lafayette may need us to scout the other roads, Sam."

Sam did not answer.

"Sam!" Jeremiah said, turning around. "Sam!"

His friend was gone. "He's lost," thought Jeremiah frantically. "I'll go back and find him." No, he couldn't now. He had to get to camp with news of the enemy in case Captain McLane for some reason didn't. But Sam! How could he just go off and leave Sam? He would hurry, he decided, run all the way to camp and then return.

The sky was just beginning to brighten when he reached Lafayette. Captain McLane had already informed the young Frenchman of the enemy's three-pronged movement. Jeremiah need not have left Sam after all. He would go right back down Ridge Road and find him.

The Marquis, however, had other plans.

"We are two thousand to their ten thousand. Retreat and rendezvous across the river," he deliberated. "It must be accomplished. But by which road? Our scouts must discover a safe route and quickly!" His slender figure grew taut with the realization of near disaster. He turned to Jeremiah. "Sam must find his way back alone, for I need every scout. You, Jeremy, search the terrain to the north."

With the sinking knowledge that he must abandon his friend, Jeremiah obeyed. After hearing from one of the sergeants that the British were reported to be advancing rapidly, he broke into a run. One third of the Americans' army was here at Barren Hill, the "new" army, well trained

"He has found him! Look!"

by Baron Von Steuben, better clothed and fed at last because of General Greene's work as quartermaster. They must not be captured!

Jeremiah ran through some bushes and out onto a road he had not seen before. This road seemed to end abruptly a little way to his left. As he followed it he saw that it did not end but dropped sharply down the hill and followed the riverbank to a good fording place. The army could disappear from sight and march along this road concealed by the height of the hill!

His lungs seemed ready to burst when he finally reached the Marquis with the news of his discovery.

Lafayette quickly sent out a small force to make the British think he planned attack, not retreat. Then he ordered the main part of his army to march down the hill and out of sight.

Jeremiah stood glumly by the Marquis as the rear guard regrouped and prepared to complete the successful retreat. "General Lafayette," he said, "about the scout—"

"Yes, yes. One of Captain McLane's Indians is looking for him. Ah, *voilà!* He has found him! Look!"

Sam was being supported up the hill by a tall Oneida. As they drew closer Jeremiah could see that though he tried hard to smile, his straw-colored hair was matted with blood. "There's my friend," Sam gasped.

When the Indian approached, Jeremiah took Sam's other arm and they started off.

When they had reached safety on the other side of the river, the Indian, to Jeremiah's surprise said: "You are

Colonel Knox's boy. I am sure now. We meet again. This is your friend, that is good. I have saved his life, as you saved mine many moons ago."

The painted copper face crinkled into a smile and Jeremiah shouted, "Doah-darie-yagey!"

"Ah," declared the young Marquis, "where else but in America could such a thing happen? Is it any wonder the moment I heard of your country I loved her? But come. The three British armies are about to meet. Much as I would like to watch while they close their trap on empty air, we must get safely back to Valley Forge. This, my friends, was a narrow escape!"

Later, Jeremiah recounted the story to General Knox.

"One third of our force!" exclaimed Henry. "What a tragedy that would have been, for, as you probably have guessed, General Washington hopes to take not only Philadelphia but General Clinton's entire army. It could mean the end of the war. Keep your rifle ready, Jeremy. The Marquis has asked for your services in this 'grand operation' as he calls it."

Chapter 19

A MONTH PASSED, and still the "grand operation" did not begin. The grumbling in camp grew when it was learned that Philadelphia was completely evacuated and General Clinton's troops, vans, and fieldpieces were moving east toward the sea. Ten thousand soldiers were escaping to British-held New York! The old plan of splitting the colonies in two by thrusting up the Hudson River would again become a possibility. Still no marching orders came for the well-trained, eager men in Valley Forge.

After meeting Doah-darie-yagey, Jeremiah had learned that Rifleman Thompson had been in camp for several days with Morgan's riflemen. "Yep," the gruff Virginian had explained. "Doah just joined his tribesmen for that one time at Barren Hill. Regularly he's with Morgan, like me. We sorta teamed up at Saratoga under old Dan. Doah fires while I load, then I fire while he loads. Worked out the scheme at Oriskany. You see, boy, I tried to get Doah back to his tribe after you left to catch the artillery train, and it weren't long before we got mixed up in that Mohawk Valley fighting."

Now Jeremiah watched Thompson's whittling knife glitter in the blazing June sunshine.

"You never did get back to Virginia, sir, did you?"

"Nope, we're fighting our way south, you could say, me and the Oneida. He's got no village to go back to. The Mohawks took care of that! So he's sticking with me and Morgan. Never did think I'd take so to an Indian." The growling laugh sounded. "Doah's all right, all right."

"Sam thinks so too," Jeremiah commented. "Poor fellow, he must be back in Worcester by now convalescing."

Thompson stood up and stretched. "This here waiting," he complained. "What's holding us up? Thought we was going to scoop up them Redcoats, baggage 'n' all, and here we are letting them get away, clean away."

In a few days Thompson had less cause for complaint. Morgan's men were sent to cover General Clinton's movements and Lafayette was given command of the first attacking force. General Washington would follow with the main part of the army, including General Knox and his artillery company.

When Jeremiah reported to the young Frenchman he found him elated at this unexpected honor, an important command with good fighting men. It was unexpected, Jeremiah discovered, because the experienced General Charles Lee had been offered the post first. He had refused, stating bluntly that American soldiers were no match for Redcoats and Hessians.

Lafayette seemed to have no doubts, Jeremiah thought, as he rode behind the young Frenchman and General Wayne.

"We shall camp at Englishtown," the Marquis said to Wayne.

Wayne nodded in agreement. "From there we can send out our scouts. The British are supposedly at Monmouth Courthouse. That's about five miles southeast of Englishtown."

"Excellent, excellent!"

They were soon encamped at Englishtown. Jeremiah's militia shirt had been soaked through several times, by sweat, rain, sweat, rain, and now by sweat again. The meadows were steaming as the hot sun beat down on the rain-drenched earth.

When he saw a rain-swollen stream behind the camp he pulled off his shirt, lay flat on his stomach, and gratefully sloshed his head and shoulders with the murky water.

The splashing water must have muffled the approaching hoofbeats, he realized later, for he first knew he was not alone when a surly voice commanded: "Take me to the Frenchman! Well, boy, don't gape! Hurry! I am taking over this command. General Washington's orders."

General Charles Lee glared down from his mount. He was as sullen faced as the day Jeremiah had accidentally bumped into him in Vassal House hall two and a half years before. A flash of dislike for the rude Lee made Jeremiah remember Lucy's words, "He's shifty-eyed. I don't trust him." But General Washington evidently did. There was nothing a volunteer aide-de-camp could do but obey.

Jeremiah noticed how well Lafayette hid what must be acute disappointment. Graciously he turned over his command to the older man, showing no resentment. But the men were resentful. Were they to be led by a general who had no faith in them? Some hinted darkly that Lee would protect the British departure, not attack!

On the evening of June 27, Jeremiah made known his dissatisfaction to one of General Wayne's aides, a red-headed Pennsylvanian about his own age.

"The British are covered on the left by Dickinson and on the right by Morgan. General Washington is to our rear, but General Lee delays. Doesn't he want us to win?"

"Careful. That kind of talk could land you in the prison barracks, but," he winked, "I agree with you."

All through the night Jeremiah could not sleep. The sound of Clinton's loaded wagons creaking slowly eastward could clearly be heard. Still no orders came from General Lee.

Finally, at seven o'clock the next morning, the camp came alive. They were marching to Monmouth Court-house. The attack was at last under way.

Jeremiah, his rifle over his shoulder, swung into step behind the three regiments which Lafayette had been given to command. He, with another volunteer, a lanky young farmer, pulled a small fieldpiece behind them.

"What's the plan?" Jeremiah asked his companion.

"No plan. That's the whole trouble, General Wayne says. No plan at all. General Lee called a meeting, I hear, but all he said was 'move cautiously.' "

"Caution?" Jeremiah exclaimed. "I'd say we need bold-ness now!"

"Mebbe, but you ain't runnin' this shindig."

Word sifted back that the last of the British had left

Monmouth. Clinton was gone but there was still hope of capturing his rear guard. General Wayne had attacked and he was calling for more men.

The rising clouds of dust made it impossible to see, and the shouted commands, "Move forward!" "Move back!" were impossible to distinguish. Jeremiah left the fieldpiece with his lanky companion and ran to the front where Lafayette stood conferring with General Wayne's aide.

"Jeremy," said the Frenchman, "stay with me. We're moving these regiments forward to assist General Wayne."

In good order they marched double time until they reached Wayne's position. Jeremiah could see the familiar scarlet coats of the British. No green-coated Hessians were about.

The British infantry fell back suddenly and a fury of galloping cavalrymen charged forward. Jeremiah drew back his hammer. He obeyed the shouted commands to "Hold fire!" then "Fire!" A deafening roar, smoke and flame, and the horses, many riderless, plunged back through the lines, leaving the half-beaten British infantry exposed once more.

"Back!" came the order from the mounted General Lee.

"A new position, no doubt, to await new attacking orders," explained Lafayette. "Back!" he shouted, repeating Lee's order.

But no orders for attack came. General Lee trotted up once more. "Retire in order. Retire, I say!"

"General—" Lafayette protested, though he started to regroup his men for retreat as commanded.

"It is obvious," said General Lee with a self-satisfied smirk, "that we cannot stand against them."

"But General Lee," Jeremiah called out, "we are standing—and winning!"

Lee stared down coldly. "Your name?"

"Jeremiah Cutler."

"You will report to my tent after this ridiculous expedition is over and take the consequences for your insolent insubordination."

"General Lee," Lafayette pleaded, "it is most natural in the heat of battle, I entreat you, sir—"

General Lee's mouth curled into a sneer. "Your plea is touching, sir. Cutler, report to my quarters later as directed!"

Jeremiah felt the Marquis' touch on his shoulder as he answered, "Yes, General Lee."

As the retreat began, the heat soared. Jeremiah followed Lafayette whose face was beaded with perspiration. Some of the older men dropped by the roadside, overcome. Others wandered distractedly, asking the same question over and over, "Why? Why are we retreating?"

"Why, General Lafayette?" Jeremiah asked with a sinking feeling in the pit of his stomach. Not only was the battle over, but his military career as well. General Lee was second in command to General Washington. One word from him would be enough to send him back home in disgrace, or perhaps to prison. "We had them, sir," he insisted. "Why are we giving up?"

Lafayette shook his head wearily, then he suddenly

straightened and squinted as he looked down the English-town road. Jeremiah could feel the Frenchman's heavy rings biting deep into his flesh as he grasped his shoulder.

"Look!" said the Marquis in an awed whisper.

Jeremiah looked. All he could see was a cloud of dust. Had the British somehow encircled them? He shaded his eyes and looked again. A white horse was charging through the swirling cloud of dust.

"General Washington!" he cried.

"It is!" said the Marquis as the galloping white horse pranced to a halt beside General Lee's mount. "Jeremy, listen!" General Washington's voice pierced through the dust and heat. "At last he sees General Lee for what he really is. Listen! What a *vocabulaire!* Ah, *magnifique!*"

Jeremiah listened. Everyone was listening—joyfully. The Jersey air which had crackled for two days with summer storms now crackled anew with General Washington's un-leashed anger! This then, thought Jeremiah, was the light-ning temper which the Virginia farmer-fox hunter tightened his lips against. It was, as the Marquis said, *magnifique!*

The men cheered! They shouted! The Commander in Chief could not doubt their wholehearted agreement. General Wayne quickly and furiously reported what had hap-pened: the men had been forced to retreat while winning— by General Charles Lee!

With renewed spirit the regiments re-formed. Just in time, for the encouraged Redcoats were pressing close be-hind them.

General Wayne volunteered to hold the line until the

divisions regrouped. Henry's artillery was wheeled into place on both sides. Baron Von Steuben looked on approvingly. General Greene's division marched up to General Washington's right. General Stirling stood ready with his men on the left. Lafayette took command of the second line.

"We are ready!" cried Lafayette exultantly.

As the fighting grew fiercer, the heat became even more intense. Jeremiah fired, reloaded, fired, or held fire as commanded. His throat was dry and choked with dust. His hat disappeared during a fast skirmish. His eyes burned and perspiration trickled down his back.

The British attacked, the left wing, the right. The American cannon belched and roared. The British fell back, then regrouped and closed up in a precise line. A cannon ball cut across that line, knocking all their muskets to the ground.

Finally the sun set and the Redcoats, far from beaten, withdrew. Darkness prevented a new American attack.

Lafayette threw himself full length under a tree. Jeremiah sat beside him. "At dawn tomorrow," the Marquis said sleepily, "we shall surround them."

Jeremiah pressed his back against the tree trunk. He remembered with a jolt General Lee's order to report to his tent.

The drowsy Frenchman had evidently just remembered too. He laughed and said, "General Lee ordered you to report to him, remember? Ah, Jeremy, it is the General himself who will have to do some reporting. He is being court-martialed."

Jeremiah sighed with relief and weariness. He slid down and curled up on the grass beneath the tree.

Something woke him in the night and he rolled over and opened his eyes. What he saw made him blink and then smile contentedly. Two figures were sleeping next to him—the young Marquis and General George Washington himself.

Chapter 20

ON THE NEXT day the British were not surrounded and captured, for they had slipped to safety during the night. The war, it seemed, would drag on and on.

The old threat of a British attack up the Hudson River loomed again. Yet an attack on the strong British position in New York was impossible. Always there was the formidable British Navy. The strong British positions in the South must be considered too.

The war simmered almost to a standstill during the summer of 1778. General Washington semicircled the lower New York area by spreading his camps from Connecticut to the Hudson River Highlands, to Morristown, New Jersey, and, of course, Philadelphia was now well within American lines.

To Jeremiah, Philadelphia in October, 1778, was the place where a dream came true. Not only did he receive one of the new blue uniforms sent over from France, but an ensign's commission as well.

"You have earned this honor." Henry had just administered the officer's oath of allegiance to his former apprentice, and his cheeks were flushed with pride. "I know you will serve your country and your superior officers admirably."

During the winter of 1778–1779, Jeremiah did just that. He could be depended upon to carry speedily the important messages which kept the sprawling camps in touch with General Washington's Headquarters near Morristown. He was in the saddle, his long rifle under his knee, most of his waking hours.

The following spring, at the end of May, he performed an errand in Philadelphia for a superior officer which disturbed him. But he told no one, because, after thinking it over, he decided it was unimportant.

In his saddlebag, as he rode into Philadelphia this May morning, were several sealed letters to General Arnold. The General and Peggy, his bride of a few weeks, were living luxuriously in the Penn Mansion. They had liveried servants and expensive furnishings, and former merchant Arnold was said to be engaged in business transactions. It had been hinted by prominent people that General Arnold might be using army funds for private trading and he had angrily demanded a hearing from Congress to clear his name. His wish had been granted. Jeremiah knew Henry Knox had been chosen to be on the Board of Inquiry, a task he found distasteful. This was the subject of some of the letters in his saddlebag.

One of the letters to General Arnold conveyed General Knox's warm congratulations on his recent marriage. "I hope it will also convey my full confidence in him," he had told Jeremiah. "Gossip! Malicious gossip! General Arnold is an honest merchant. His wounded leg keeps him from active duty and his enormous energy finds an outlet in trading again. Certainly I would turn to bookselling in like circumstances. I am glad he has challenged the gossipers. He will clear his name, never fear."

Some of the communications Jeremiah carried were about renewed British activity in New York. Were they planning to move up the Hudson River? General Washington was shifting his army's strength to the Hudson area once more. West Point was being strongly fortified.

On this blossom-scented spring morning Jeremiah dismounted in front of the Penn Mansion. One of the Arnold servants hurried to hold his horse, another escorted him to the front door, another led him down the hall and asked him to wait. "A moment, sir, if you please."

Jeremiah unbuckled his dispatch case as he was shown into a large, airy room. He walked toward the seated General Arnold. "From Headquarters, sir." He placed the packet of letters near the blue-broadcloth elbow.

To Jeremiah's amazement, General Arnold reacted as though it were a packet of exploding gunpowder. With one sweeping gesture he sent the letters swirling to the floor. His lips quivered and his eyes contracted to needle points.

"What do you bring me, sir? More accusations?" he shouted.

A servant rushed in, carrying a cut-glass water carafe and a small brown bottle. "Mrs. Arnold, sir, wants you to take your medicine."

"Thank you," the General said calmly. "Thank Mrs.

Arnold for her kind attention," he called as the servant departed.

Jeremiah stood shifting his feet, hoping to be dismissed quickly. His glance flickered nervously over the General's paper-scattered desk. A framed charcoal portrait of an elaborately dressed young woman with a towering headdress caught his eye. This, he thought, must be the Philadelphia-born Mrs. Arnold. In the corner of the portrait the artist had scrawled his name. Jeremiah squinted. It looked like André. John André was the British officer who, Henry had said, had arranged the lavish farewell party for General Howe right here in Philadelphia. No doubt this same artistic Englishman had sketched the then Peggy Shippen as well. André. He must ask Henry if he ever had found out whether this André was the same one who had shared their Lake George hut almost three and a half years ago.

General Arnold muttered a half apology for his outburst. "It's this blasted idleness," he said.

"Yes, sir," Jeremiah had always admired Arnold's ability as a soldier, but when he learned that the cocky Connecticut merchant sent money regularly to Dr. Warren's children his admiration had deepened to near hero worship. "May I say, General, that I have long been an admirer of yours."

The General smiled with his mouth, but his eyes kept their strange sharp glitter.

"My secretary across the hall will give you my communications to Headquarters. You may go, sir."

Jeremiah turned smartly and walked toward the door.

"One moment, Ensign," called the General. "Cutler, is it?"

"Yes, sir."

"Ensign Cutler, I wonder if you would be so kind as to deliver a personal letter for me to a party on Front Street?"

"Of course, sir. I'd be happy to."

He waited as the General's pen flew. The portrait by André again caught his eye. That's why, he decided later, he made the blunder which touched off another tantrum. Jeremiah took the sealed letter.

"Ensign, take this to Stansbury, the glass and china dealer. You needn't wait for an answer. Just tell him it's a further inquiry into the china collection of the late John Anderson. Mrs. Arnold is quite a fancier of old china." There was an abrupt little laugh. "Now, sir. It's Stansbury's shop on Front Street. You have it all quite clear?"

"Yes, General Arnold. I am to deliver this to a Mr. Stansbury on Front Street and tell him it's a further inquiry into the collection of the late John André."

The General jumped to his feet and pounded his desk with both clenched fists. "I said quite distinctly John A-n-d-e-r-s-o-n—Anderson!"

Jeremiah felt his own face flaming with embarrassment. "Sir, sir—" he stammered.

The enraged General cut him short. He leaned across the desk. The veins in his neck bulged. Looking straight at Jeremiah he said in a low tense voice, "Why did you say that? Why? I demand to know!"

"General Arnold, please, sir. I don't know why." Jeremiah hesitated, then quickly added the explanation he suddenly realized was true. "It must have been because I was admiring that portrait on your desk. I noted the artist's name, André. A slip of the tongue, General. André, Anderson. The names are similar, sir."

The General lowered himself slowly into his chair. He mopped his brow and turned to Jeremiah apologetically. "The portrait, of course, the names are similar. It was a most natural mistake. You are quite right. I beg you, forgive my outburst. These idle days play havoc with my nerves. I would appreciate it, sir, should you forget this incident entirely."

Jeremiah leaned forward and said sincerely, "General Arnold, the entire matter is as though it had never been, I assure you."

The General seemed mollified. "Never mind the letter to Stansbury. No," he said when Jeremiah protested, "I have no right really to ask you to deliver my personal letters."

Jeremiah's sympathy went out to the man drooped in his chair, spent after his moment of fury. "Please, sir, I would consider it an honor to be of service to you."

"Very well then, and thank you."

After Jeremiah delivered the letter which had caused such a commotion, he rode down Front Street and passed a small open carriage drawn at a lively clip by a chestnut mare.

"Jeremiah!" The high clear call made him rein in abruptly and turn around.

"It's Nancy, Jeremiah," said the blonde young lady in the carriage as he trotted back. "Don't you know me? I must confess I might not have known you, but I heard through Miss Betsy, who heard through Major Hamilton, that a certain Ensign Cutler could be relied upon to carry messages to and from Philadelphia. Oh, I just knew it must be you, Jeremiah!"

"Nancy!" he exclaimed. Jeremiah swept off his hat. "You look, well, different."

Nancy patted the high blonde curls at the back of her head. "I'm sixteen now, could that be why?" Then her eyes twinkled and she said in a rush, "Oh, Jeremiah, I'm not different, not really, and neither is Rebel. See."

He quickly dismounted. The harnessed chestnut mare was Rebel. He patted her soft nose and she tossed her head away from him. "She doesn't know me any more." In swift succession came old memories—Concord, Lexington, New York, Albany. It all seemed so long ago. "Rebel doesn't remember," he said softly.

"She'll get used to you again," Nancy said.

"No. You deserve to keep her. Besides, she couldn't stand hard riding any more." He reached out to pat her again and she nuzzled against his shoulder. "See," he laughed, "she's thanking me for leaving her with you."

"Oh, Jeremiah. Tell me everything! Your last letter said you were going with General Knox as a volunteer. It was by chance I learned you were an officer. I think it's just wonderful! I'm here in Philadelphia," she rushed on, "with Miss Betsy. She's sweet on Major Hamilton and besides,

General Schuyler is sitting with Congress. I only have a year to go before my service is up. Of course, I'm satisfied to stay with the Schuylers. I'm more like a companion now than a servant. I fix Miss Betsy's hair and write letters sometimes for Mrs. Schuyler." Nancy gasped for breath. "Oh, Jeremiah, you look so handsome in your uniform. Do you think I've grown to be just a little pretty? Don't say so unless you really mean it, now. You know, I started reading *Robinson Crusoe* for the sixteenth time. My, he got himself into a mess almost with those cannibals. I know he gets away, but every time I read it I'm afraid they'll eat him. Tell me, do you still think about the coffee house-bookstore. Oh dear, won't the British ever leave New York? Jeremiah, did I make any mistakes in those letters I sent you? My, it is wonderful to see you again!"

Jeremiah laughed as Nancy leaned back against the carriage seat and fanned herself with a lace-edged handkerchief. She was completely out of breath.

"You haven't changed, Nancy. I'm so glad. Yes, you are, not just a little pretty, but very pretty. As for all those other questions, I couldn't begin to answer them. I have to get back to Headquarters. But, yes, about the mistakes in your letters. Spell *general*," he teased.

"G-e-n-e-r-a-l. You see, I fooled you, Jeremiah," Nancy cried. "I'm learning all the time."

"I have to get back to Jersey, Nancy," he said, "but I will write."

"Send it upriver. We're leaving for home soon. We never do have time to talk, you and I."

After mounting, he reined in next to her carriage. She stared at his black horse.

He smiled. "Do you want this horse instead of Rebel?"

"Oh, goodness, no." She tossed her bright curls and looked up at him. The patched sunlight flickered through the trees, over her pert nose and firm little chin. She was very pretty, he decided.

"I was just thinking that I saw a horse exactly like yours hitched to the post in front of that Tory china shop down the street." She laughed. "Don't look so alarmed. I know it wasn't yours. You wouldn't traffic with Stansbury and his like. He crosses the line into New York with honest businessmen. Neither we nor the British want honest trading stopped, but everybody in Philadelphia knows Stansbury trades more than china. He's a spy, but they just can't catch him at it."

A touch of the reins across Rebel's back and she was gone.

Jeremiah let his horse clop slowly down the street. That letter from General Arnold to Stansbury. It bothered him. Should he go back and warn the General about the china dealer's reputation? But Nancy had said "everyone in Philadelphia knew about Stansbury." Should he tell someone else? Henry? No, General Knox would be outraged. Was Jeremiah, as so many others, questioning Arnold's business dealings? Jeremiah wouldn't want him to think he could ever forget the country's debt to Arnold's bravery. Suppose, he thought, the former merchant's trading was taking him, unknowingly, of course, into contact with a British spy.

Shouldn't he be warned? But he couldn't imagine even Henry broaching the subject to fiery General Arnold.

If only he could discuss it with someone! Thompson, for instance, with his gruff, wise observations. But the Virginian was not heading south as he had hoped, but north. He and the Oneida, under Morgan, were sweeping the Mohawk Valley clear of Tories and Indian scalping parties.

That made him think of Nancy again. He was thankful she had escaped those Indian raids. She was safe, and how good it was to find that she hadn't really changed! She still chattered away. She still said exactly what she meant. She had been very serious about the "Tory china shop."

"But," Jeremiah thought, as he left Philadelphia behind him and heeled his horse into a trot, "she was only repeating what someone else had said, just some gossiper!" He would keep the entire affair to himself.

Chapter 21

PRESENTLY Jeremiah was on his way to New Windsor, a camp ten miles north of West Point on the Hudson River. But by September, a few weeks before his nineteenth birthday, he was on the move again, this time to Connecticut, and it was no longer Ensign, but Lieutenant Cutler under Major Benjamin Tallmadge of the 2nd Continental Dragoons.

The long hard hours in the saddle had helped earn him this honor, Henry said. Good horsemanship was a necessary qualification for a galloping, dark-blue-jacketed, helmeted dragoon, of course. But, Major Tallmadge demanded more of his men—intelligence, daring, and a cautious tongue. For Major Tallmadge was head of the Secret Service.

Across Long Island Sound from the north shore of Long Island to the south shore of Connecticut, that was the route of important information gathered by Patriots in British-held New York. From Setauket, Long Island, across the water under cover of night, to Fairfield, Connecticut. From this point Major Tallmadge's dragoons relayed the vital messages to General Washington wherever he might be at the time.

On the day he left New Windsor, Jeremiah gave three letters to General Knox—one to William, one to Sam, and one to Nancy, telling of his promotion, not, of course, the nature of his duties.

On the last day of September, 1779, he reported to Major Tallmadge.

"Sit down, Lieutenant," said Major Tallmadge after giving Jeremiah a firm handshake. "Now look at this letter and see what you make of it."

Jeremiah read the fine writing:

To John Bolton, Esq.
Knowing of your past ventures, it may interest you to hear that my client has £5000 ready to invest in a whaling fleet.

> *Yr humble servant*
> *Samuel Culper, Jr.*

Jeremiah looked up, puzzled, and Major Tallmadge smiled.

"A harmless business letter," the Major said. "Well, Lieutenant, that's the sort of information you'll risk your neck for. Let me explain. I am John Bolton, £5000 are British soldiers, the whaling fleet means they are embarking, probably to protect the West Indies from the French, but they could be headed for one of our seaports. That, we'll find out later. In the meantime, General Washington will know there's movement afoot."

"And Culper, Jr., is our intelligence agent in New York," Jeremiah said. The harmless business letter made sense now.

"Exactly, Lieutenant! Usually we use a more complicated code than this," he said, tapping the letter. "Only Culper, whose name isn't Culper, of course, and I know the key. But this will show you the importance of our mission. Every bit of information must get through to General Washington, even the wild rumors. Why, just last week we were told that Ethan Allen was going over to the British! Wishful thinking by His Majesty's officers, it developed, but it was nevertheless reported to General Washington." The Major leaned back in his chair. "As a dragoon, that will be your job. You'll push through rain and snow to get these messages through. But tonight, you'll ride with me to the source of our information."

Jeremiah stood up, his crested helmet under his left arm. He saluted smartly and smiled. "Yes, sir!"

After dark he and the Major rode swiftly toward the Fairfield beaches. They reined in near a sandy bluff. The Major dismounted and handed him his reins, then he walked toward the shore.

Jeremiah waited. Not a star brightened the blackness of water and sky. The Major's slim figure became a smudged shadow.

Suddenly the horses, both dappled gray stallions, pawed the ground. Jeremiah tightened his grip on the reins and listened. The slap, slap of water against the side of some moving craft was unmistakable.

A boat ground into the sand with a sharp rasping swish, and the shadow of a cloaked figure mingled with the Major's.

The shadows parted. Another swish, and the rhythmic slap of water began again, becoming fainter and fainter as the Major walked back toward Jeremiah.

"Tomorrow you'll ride to Headquarters with this," he said. They urged their horses back toward camp. "Nothing startling or new about this bit of information. General Clinton, as always, is searching for a way to capture West Point."

It became routine for Jeremiah to ride from Connecticut to the Hudson and across to Morristown, New Jersey, during the winter of 1779–1780. A bitter winter it was. Blizzards howled, food was scarce. Even a bit of salt meat was hard to find. The various states made fewer and fewer contributions to the Continental Army. People were tired of war. Independence threatened to become a shattered hope, especially after 8500 British soldiers landed in Charleston, South Carolina's seaport.

According to Nancy the winter in Albany had been just as bad. One spring day, when Jeremiah returned from the almost destitute Morristown camp to Connecticut, he found a letter from her waiting for him.

April 15, 1780

Dear Lieutenant Jeremiah,

I didn't answer your letter because I knew it would never get through. We have been near buried in snow all winter. But now I feel like the robin outside my window. I am free! I feel free too, because I am going somewhere—to Philadelphia!

As I told Miss Betsy, on the day my indenture ended I didn't feel free because I had no place to go. She laughed. I was glad. I didn't want her to think I didn't like it here. She said she thought she understood. Would I like to go to Philadelphia, she asked. Mrs. Arnold had a new baby I could help care for. Miss Betsy and Mrs. Schuyler became well acquainted with Mrs. Arnold last year in Philadelphia. Miss Betsy said she would write a letter telling how handy I was and ask Mrs. Arnold to hire me as a special favor—and she did!

So I expect I will be in Philadelphia by the time you receive this. Mrs. Arnold is not apt to refuse because her husband, General Arnold, asked our General Schuyler to help him get the post he wants at West Point.

If the Arnolds go to West Point, and if they keep me as a nursemaid, and if you stay where you are in Connecticut, we won't be very far apart. If you get some time to yourself, maybe you could come to see me.

Yr friend,

Free Nancy Star

Jeremiah put off answering the letter because he, in company with another dragoon, went on continuous scouting duty during the spring and early summer in the neutral area between the two armies. Down Hardscrabble Road, past Chappaqua, over to the Hudson's eastern bank, back to White Plains, and east along the Connecticut south shore, he and his fellow dragoon would ride, their pistols holstered to either side of their saddles, their long swords sheathed and buckled at their sides. (Jeremiah's long rifle now hung over his bunk, ready to be used in an emergency.) It was a hazardous route because of the ruffian bands which roamed the area. These outlaws knew loyalty neither to British nor to Americans. Their only aim was to rob innocent travelers or to capture information to sell to either army.

During the summer of 1780 the American cause began to look black. Charleston, South Carolina, had been captured and the entire South was spread before the British Army, ready for the taking.

Then good news followed bad. The French were landing crack troops in Newport, Rhode Island. Major Tallmadge scarcely had sent off this bit of intelligence when one of his men brought him terrible tidings. From Culper, Jr., across Long Island Sound, had come word of British soldiers, thousands of them, embarking from western Long Island's north shore. They planned to sail out the Sound to the ocean, thence to Newport, and take the entire French army by surprise.

Immediately after the two dragoons, who had swiftly transmitted this information to General Washington, returned to Connecticut, Jeremiah was called into Major Tallmadge's office.

"We have our orders from General Washington. You, Lieutenant Cutler, must do a bit of acting." He handed him three sealed letters. "Now, there are three Tory houses in the neutral area we know of." He spread a rough map out on the table and pointed. "Here, here, and here. You are to drop these accidentally. Make a great show of galloping by, as though you were on a life and death errand, which, in fact, you are."

"Yes, sir. These are false American plans then."

"Exactly. It's all a bluff, a bluff which General Washington hopes and prays will succeed. Our Commander in Chief is making a great many obvious movements, pretending an attack on New York. He hopes to worry the British into calling off their attack on Newport. When you return, Cutler, join me on the Fairfield beach."

Jeremiah, the letters tucked in his vest, galloped off.

He reached the first Tory farmhouse. A woman was in the yard, weeding a vegetable patch. She looked up as he rode by. He slipped one of the letters under his knee, then he jerked on the reins, pretending his mount had shied at something in the road. A great struggle went on as he sawed at the reins. He would see that his poor frantic horse received an extra bag of oats later to compensate for this rough treatment. The gray stallion reared and snorted. Finally, Jeremiah quieted him and rode off, letting the false document flutter to the ground.

He could imagine the woman's crafty dash into the road to get the letter, but he dared not look back.

The second false message was "lost" in front of a white-washed stone house near Tarrytown, where an old man leaned on his fence blinking in the sun and watched the blue-jacketed dragoon struggle with his frantic, shying mount.

Before he reached the third appointed Tory house in

White Plains, Jeremiah stopped beside a little brook. He dismounted, loosened the cinch strap on his lathered horse and walked him a few minutes before allowing him to drink. The third false message was safely tucked inside his jacket. He had accomplished two thirds of his mission ahead of schedule, so he felt only a little guilty about taking this brief moment of relaxation.

But just a few minutes later he regretted the snatched moment in the quiet forest, for behind him came the rustling beat of approaching horses.

One of the outlaw bands! He could see their masked faces now, and he dashed toward his horse to get his pistols, but it was too late. His arms were pinned behind his back and a kerchief was stuffed in his mouth.

"How I have waited and waited for the day you would scout this area alone. You were bound to grow careless," said a voice, a strangely familiar, haughty voice.

Jeremiah felt his arms being expertly tied behind him and he could hear the stamping of several horses as they reined in among the trees.

A masked figure, wearing a long black coat and a broad-brimmed black hat, stood before him.

"Helmet, blue jacket, polished boots. Fine feathers for a bookseller's sweeper boy!"

The tall black figure pulled down his mask. Jeremiah's brain reeled with the astonishment his gagged mouth could not cry—Roger! It couldn't be, but it was—Roger.

Chapter 22

"REMOVE THE GAG!" Roger imperiously ordered.

Two ragged, masked figures rushed forward. One pulled the wadded kerchief from Jeremiah's mouth. The other unbuckled his sword.

"I claim that, and the horse and pistols." Roger held out his hand for the sword.

The ragged man snarled a protest, but turned over the sword to his leader.

"You're not in uniform," Jeremiah blurted when he caught his breath. "You could be taken as a spy and hanged."

"Uniform?" asked Roger inspecting the sword. "Oh, that red coat I used to wear, you mean. I discarded that last year. I couldn't get a decent command. And do you know Lord Percy took my wild life essays to England when he sailed. They rated not so much as a thank you from the Queen, let alone a title. It was all most maddening indeed."

"You're the leader of an outlaw band, aren't you, Roger? And your loyalty belongs to neither side." In spite of what Henry had told him, Jeremiah found this hard to believe.

"Loyalty?" Roger said flippantly. "Loyalty, a noble word. But what is it really now? Can you see it? Can you hold it in your hand? Like solid coin, for example?"

Jeremiah sputtered, "Roger!"

"The bookseller's sweeper boy is shocked. Dear me!" Roger's eyes narrowed. "You're a fool if you think you've advanced yourself. You will always be a sweeper boy! Do you hear? A sweeper boy!"

Jeremiah clenched his jaws. "Very well. Get on with this. What's to become of me?" It was lucky Roger hadn't captured him when he carried real plans. Like the other outlaws he would turn them over to the British—for a price.

"Search him!" commanded Roger. "You see how they do my bidding." He smiled vainly. "I am commander and king to my men."

The ruffians cleaned out Jeremiah's pockets, his watch, his money. They even ripped the buttons off his coat. One pounced upon the sealed letter in his pocket.

"I shall take care of that," said Roger. He broke the seal and read. "Hmmm, an attack on New York by General Washington. The British will want this bit of information and they shall have it for—say, £500."

"Well?" Jeremiah demanded angrily to cover his satisfaction. The false message would no doubt be channeled directly to the top command of the British army. "What are you going to do with me?" Roger couldn't, he wouldn't order him killed. Or would he? I won't show any fear. At least I'll try not to.

Roger pocketed the letter. He stared down haughtily

at Jeremiah, who stared back, until Roger, uneasily, looked away. In that split second Jeremiah thought he could see the old Roger, the one who had fished and sailed with him years before in Boston's Back Bay.

"Untie him!" Roger wheeled his horse around. "Get the pistols, but let him have the horse." He tapped his breast pocket. "This message will bring in coin enough to buy fifty horses."

The binding ropes were swiftly cut. Jeremiah was free, and Roger and his outlaw band galloped off, disappearing among the trees.

Jeremiah brushed his buttonless jacket and mounted. Circling about he rode along the Connecticut shore toward Fairfield.

Major Tallmadge and two of his dragoons were reined in under a tree. Their faces were tense as they watched a giant flotilla in the Sound sailing east toward the ocean and the French army at Newport.

After quickly explaining his disheveled appearance, Jeremiah joined in the watching and waiting. All through the night they stayed by the shore, taking turns at catching a little sleep.

The next afternoon Major Tallmadge said, "There's nothing we can do. The ruse has obviously failed."

Jeremiah shaded his eyes against the sun. Across the sparkling water he thought he saw—was it?—a whaling fleet? No!

"Major," he said, "look! British ships! The bluff worked. They're coming back, every one of them."

Weary but happy they rode back to camp. The French army at Newport had been saved.

Jeremiah stretched out in his bunk. How he wished he could tell someone about this successful venture, William, Sam, or Nancy, but he couldn't. The ruse might have to be used again.

And he wouldn't tell anyone about Roger. He hated even to think of him. He had seen Roger's fate in the murderous way his own men looked at his turned back. Solid coin! In the end it would be his undoing. Jeremiah could see it all. A squabble over some captured loot, the lightning thrust of a dagger, Roger in a crumpled, lifeless heap, his murderer proclaiming himself the new leader of the ruffian band.

Why had Roger become what he was? What would Nancy say? Would she wonder, as Jeremiah did, whether it was because Roger had wanted the wrong things? Or had he wanted them for the wrong reasons?

He did not write to Nancy, simply because there was nothing he could tell her, but toward the end of summer he received a letter from her, an unhappy one, from Philadelphia, which begged a favor he felt duty bound to refuse.

Philadelphia, Sept. 2, 1780

Dear Jeremiah,

We are preparing to leave for upriver. After Mrs. Arnold is settled in the Robinson house across the river from West Point I hope to leave her service, though I have not told her yet.

The baby boy is a dear little thing, but I cannot be happy with people who fly up at unexpected moments over nothing. Both General Arnold and his wife are such people.

For example, Jeremiah, how can a person get so wrought up over old dishes? Yet when a letter came about the price of some dead man's collection of china teacups, both the General and his lady flew into a tizzy. Said the General, "The terms must be better than this!" Mrs. A. went into a fit of hysterics. It was awful.

Jeremiah, I am asking a favor of you. Would you ask General Knox if I could help his lady tend her babies? I could go back to the Schuylers, but Miss Betsy might be embarrassed since she asked Mrs. Arnold specially to take me on. But, I thought, with Mrs. Knox so recently bereaved at losing one of her little girls, no one would think it amiss if she needed more help and I went to her. Mrs. Knox, I hear, is upriver too with a doctor's wife. I could get to her easy after we arrive at the Robinson house across from West Point.

I would most appreciate your kind help.

Yr friend,
Nancy

Jeremiah sat down and regretfully wrote a refusal. How could he, a mere lieutenant, he explained, interfere in the private households of two generals? But after reading his letter over, he decided it sounded unsympathetic. He tore it up. Since it was mid-September already, he reasoned, Nancy was probably already on her way with Mrs. Arnold. Major Tallmadge was taking Jeremiah and another dragoon on a scouting expedition, but they planned to be back in New Castle within a week or ten days, about the twenty-third of September. At that time he would ask for leave and go to see Nancy. He could explain to her better in person. Besides, it would be nice to talk to her again.

Just then Major Tallmadge entered. "Before we leave, Lieutenant, write out a copy of this memorandum from General Arnold. Lieutenant Colonel Jameson at Lower Salem is to give safe conduct to a business acquaintance of General Arnold's, one John Anderson."

"Yes, sir," said Jeremiah. As he wrote, the name John Anderson plagued his memory. Where had he heard that name before? Then he remembered. It was that letter he had delivered, after quite a commotion, for General Arnold. It had been to Stansbury, the Philadelphia glass and china dealer, concerning the china collection of the late John Anderson. That had been over a year ago. "Yet this John Anderson is very much alive," he puzzled. "There must be more than one John Anderson. It's not an unusual name."

Chapter 23

THE MORNING after their return to New Castle on the afternoon of September 23, Major Tallmadge called Jeremiah into his quarters. Jeremiah had never seen the Major so agitated.

"What is it, sir?"

"I don't know yet, Lieutenant. During our absence John Anderson was picked up by some militia men. He was returning from West Point and heading for New York and he carried secret papers! They were concealed in his shoe!"

"He stole secret plans from General Arnold!" exclaimed Jeremiah.

"I hope so," was the strange reply.

Jeremiah frowned, but before he could question his superior officer, the Major was hurriedly preparing to leave.

"Lieutenant Colonel Jameson has already sent word to General Arnold and he was returning John Anderson to the General at West Point, but I have ordered him brought back," said the agitated Major. "I shall take charge of this prisoner myself. The incriminating papers have been sent to General Washington who is near Hartford." The

Major pulled at his lip. "If only Jameson hadn't sent word of this capture to General Arnold," he said half to himself.

"I don't follow you, sir."

"I don't follow myself, Lieutenant. That is, I don't like the dreadful suspicion in my thoughts."

Jeremiah frowned again but said nothing.

"General Knox I understand was once your employer and benefactor. You are close friends. He is with General Washington's party, as are General Lafayette and Major Hamilton. Suppose you ride to General Arnold's house on the pretext that you are on furlough and would like to see General Knox on a personal matter when he arrives for his expected visit to Arnold."

The Robinson house where the Arnolds lived had been his planned destination, Jeremiah thought, during the furlough he had hoped to get, not to see General Knox, but to see Nancy. This peculiar turn of events made him smile. Another look at the Major's worried face made the smile disappear.

"Major," he prodded, "then what shall I do?"

"Just watch and wait. I can't tell you more than that. If nothing develops, use the pretext I mentioned as an excuse for your being at General Arnold's house. If something does—I hope I am wrong—never have I hoped more to be wrong—then state quite frankly that you are there under my orders," the Major said briskly.

In a sudden flash, as though the Major had shouted his suspicion, Jeremiah at last realized what Major Tallmadge hoped so fervently to be wrong about. He thought that General Arnold was involved in some traitorous conspiracy with the mysterious John Anderson!

All during the long ride up the eastern side of the Hudson River, he sorted and resorted a confusing jumble of jigsaw puzzle pieces. The late John Anderson's china collection, the Tory Stansbury and his china shop, Nancy's tale of Mrs. Arnold's hysterics. "Better terms," said the General. Terms, terms for what? A pass for a live John Anderson? Who was John Anderson? Terms. Terms for old china, or something far more valuable? West Point? Not West Point! General Benedict Arnold, the hero of Saratoga, the man who so generously provided for Dr. Warren's children, a traitor? Staggering! Unbelievable! Jeremiah pushed the evil thought from his mind.

He found lodgings above Fishkill. At dawn he was in the saddle again, his old rifle once more under his knee.

Nancy looked as though she couldn't believe her eyes when he halted behind the Robinson house. She was pinning pillow cases on a clothesline.

She flew to him. "Oh, Jeremiah, you've come for me!" she cried. "The housekeeper has the baby. I can leave right away. I want to get out of this awful place. Things are happening I don't understand," she chattered breathlessly, grasping both his hands as he slid to the ground.

"General Washington," she gasped, "General Lafayette, and your General Knox were expected to breakfast this morning, then Major Hamilton came and said they would be late. Then during breakfast some men in uniform, why, like yours, Jeremiah, galloped up and handed General Arnold some letters. The General went upstairs to Mrs. Arnold, then he went down again. After he left, to go across to West Point, he said, Mrs. Arnold started to cry and laugh and scream. About what, I don't know. Then General Washington came and had breakfast. Mrs. Arnold didn't even go down to see him. After he left to see General Arnold at West Point—but it turned out later that General Arnold hadn't gone to West Point at all—she began screaming that her husband was gone forever. Oh, Jeremiah," Nancy finished breathlessly, "take me away!"

"Nancy." He freed his hands from her frightened grip and shook her gently by the shoulders.

A rider approached. The girl hurried over to the dismounting soldier. "Oh, Major Hamilton, take me home to Miss Betsy!"

"Nancy," said Major Hamilton, "control yourself. Go and comfort Mrs. Arnold. She is beside herself and raving, poor lady. With good reason. Her husband's plot to turn West Point over to the British has just been exposed."

General Benedict Arnold, a traitor to his country! Jeremiah couldn't believe it. "Major Hamilton, that seems—"

The Major cut him short. "What is your mission here, Lieutenant. Pardon my abruptness, but it is hard to know whom one can trust after this."

"Major Tallmadge's orders, sir. He instructed me to wait and watch and then report back to him."

"Major Tallmadge suspected then," said Hamilton. "Now, Nancy, I shall see that you get back to the Schuylers later. In the meantime do your best to calm poor Mrs. Arnold."

"Yes, Major. I'm sorry I carried on so. It was just that I didn't understand. I think I know now— Why, Mrs. Arnold," she said slowly, her eyes widening, "knew all the time about this. She—"

"Nancy!" Major Hamilton said sharply.

"I think she did all the same," Nancy said with a proud tilt of her blonde head.

Major Hamilton, obviously annoyed, turned on his heel and left.

"Jeremiah, don't frown at me. I only said what I thought with good cause." Nancy searched his face earnestly. "We never do get time to talk. You have to go back right away I suppose."

"Yes. We're responsible for the prisoner, John Anderson."

"John Anderson!" exclaimed Nancy. "That's the man with the china teacup collection."

"Evidently he collected more than teacups," said Jeremiah grimly. "Who is he? I wonder."

Five days later Jeremiah was sent to Mabie's Tavern in Tappan where the mysterious John Anderson was being carefully guarded by Major Tallmadge's dragoons. The prisoner, it developed, was a British officer. He had been captured disguised as a civilian. This fact, along with the papers found in his shoe, made him a spy. And spies were hanged by the neck until dead.

The prisoner looked up as Jeremiah entered with a bowl

of gruel. "Come closer, Lieutenant," said John Anderson. "I have an excellent memory for faces. It is, yes, it is. Well, we meet again, but the circumstances are neither peaceful nor pleasant."

Jeremiah studied the prisoner's clear skin and friendly eyes. "We have met before?" he asked.

"Doctor Jeremiah, yes, that is the name. Have you forgotten? The Lake George hut? My festered thumb? The pocket sundial I gave you for your kind attention? Major John André, Lieutenant," he said rising to his feet, "serving his King and country to the bitter end—and proudly, sir!"

"Major André!" Jeremiah almost dropped the food he carried. Swiftly his mind flew back to that day in Philadelphia when General Arnold had asked him to deliver the letter to Stansbury. His contact with the British must have been going on then! And no wonder General Arnold had raged at that slip of the tongue. He, Jeremiah, had unknowingly spoken the real name of "the late John Anderson." The artistic Major André, Lieutenant André of the Lake George hut, and John Anderson were one and the same man!

The prisoner smiled sadly. "Tell me, Lieutenant, do you still have that sundial?"

Jeremiah, having at last recovered his composure, said, "I'm sorry, sir. I had to give it away. It saved my life and another's as well." He pictured again the wounded Oneida, his own helplessness in the snow, and the dreaded Mohawk Indians.

Major André and John Anderson were one and the same!

"Did it really? I am glad, Lieutenant." Major André interlaced his slender fingers and studied them. "A thousand sundials could not save my life now, Dr. Jeremiah. I am doomed."

Chapter 24

"THE REAL villain has escaped!" said Henry Knox to Jeremiah. They stood outside the Dutch church in the early morning sunshine.

"General Washington, gentleman that he is," continued Henry, "informed Mrs. Arnold of her husband's safe escape to British-held New York. By the way, Jeremy, Major Hamilton arranged for your little friend's safe passage up the river to the Schuylers."

At least, thought Jeremiah, Nancy was out of this miserable affair.

All the officers General Washington had assembled—Henry, Lafayette, Von Steuben, Nathanael Greene, Glover, Stark, and several others—had been conferring for hours in low, shocked whispers. The likable Major André was a spy. That meant hanging. Yet, as Henry had said, the real villain had escaped. The situation was both dismal and infuriating. There wasn't one officer, Jeremiah knew, who wouldn't prefer to see Arnold walk to the gallows instead of André.

Jeremiah shuddered in spite of the sun's warmth. "At

noon today," he said slowly, "Monday, October 2, the Major must die."

"What anguish this decision has caused us all, Jeremy," Henry said. "Perhaps I feel it more deeply because I remember, as you must, that pleasant meeting with André five years ago in the Lake George hut."

"Yes, General Knox, I remember. Will Major André be allowed his uniform? Will he be shot as he has requested?"

"His uniform, yes, but he is a spy and spies must hang. To shoot him would be to say that he is not a spy at all. However, Jeremy, General Washington sees no reason why the Major should not think he is to be shot until the very last. It might be some small comfort to him."

Ever since he learned that he was one of the dragoons chosen to escort Major John André to the gallows, Jeremiah had been unable to eat or drink. Even water choked him. And when he entered Mabie's Tavern for the last time and saw André standing erect in his uniform he wished desperately to turn and run—run far away from the gallows on the hill just outside of Tappan's town limits. Instead he gritted his teeth and marched with his fellow dragoons toward the waiting André.

"Doctor Jeremiah," chided the doomed man, "a more cheerful countenance, if you please. I am resigned to the fate that zealous duty to my King has thrust upon me."

"I can't be cheerful. Don't ask it please, Major," replied Jeremiah.

Another dragoon cleared his throat and said stiffly, "We

have grown fond of you, sir, during your short imprisonment."

The Major bowed. "Thank you, gentlemen." He adjusted the cuff of his scarlet coat and, with his eyes downcast, asked carefully, "Lieutenant Cutler, tell me, am I to be shot like a soldier, or hanged?"

Jeremiah could not utter a sound.

"I see," said the Major. "It is the gallows then."

Jeremiah dragged himself through the next nightmare hour—the sinister swinging noose, the waiting black coffin, the heartfelt prayers, the brave Major adjusting the rope about his own neck. Mercifully John André seemed to die the moment the wagon was driven out from under his feet. It was all over.

Yet it was not over, for, as Henry had said, the traitor Benedict Arnold was free. And as the weeks went by word came through the lines that Arnold was now a British Brigadier General and planned to lead his new army against the Americans in the South.

This shocking development made every American renew his vow to win independence. New vigor surged into the old cause. Every soldier forgot how tired he was of being cold and hungry. He wanted to fight!

The news made Jeremiah seethe, mostly, he guessed, because he still found the whole Arnold affair so inexplicable. It made him long to get into the Southern campaign which so many had thought a lost one, though not General Washington, and not General Greene who had accepted the command.

During one of his routine trips to Headquarters, Jeremiah asked bluntly for a transfer to the South. Henry, he knew, was sending an artillery company to North Carolina in a few weeks.

"You're a dragoon, not an artillery man," argued General Knox, "but I have heard—never mind. Next time you come I may have something definite to tell you, or perhaps I will write first to your commanding officer. That would be proper."

It was New Year's Day when Jeremiah rode into Headquarters again, hopeful that Major Tallmadge's information of three weeks before was correct. It was that he, Jeremiah Cutler, was to join Colonel Henry Lee's legion of crack cavalrymen. (Henry Lee was no relation to the discharged Charles Lee, Jeremiah was told.) Only one hundred expert horsemen with scouting experience had been chosen. Oh, let him be among them! He had already written the news to Nancy and Sam.

To his surprise, William Knox was there to greet him. They fondly clasped hands. William explained that Georgie, the sweeper boy who had replaced Jeremiah, was proving most capable. He could now manage the bookstore while William was away, and there was a new sweeper boy, Peter. "Congratulations, Captain Cutler," said his old friend.

Jeremiah was about to correct William, but just then General Henry Knox walked over. He was grinning broadly. "William, since you have said so much already, suppose I let you show Jeremy his commission papers." Like the

Henry of old he threw back his head and let out a booming laugh. He handed a legal-looking paper to William who, in turn, handed it to Jeremiah. "Yes," said Henry, "you're a captain now."

"Don't forget the other letter, Henry, and the package," chuckled William. "Sam," he called, "bring out Jeremy's package and letter."

"Sam?" exclaimed Jeremiah, turning about quickly.

"It's me," a sturdy uniformed figure shouted, running toward them. "I wasn't a very good scout, Jeremiah. I found out I was a little nearsighted. But I've become the best drummer boy ever. We'll be Sons of Liberty together again!"

"General Greene's newest drummer boy." William laughed. "Oh, yes, Sam is going South too. Now, how about the letter and package for our friend Jeremy?"

Sam scooted off.

"The fighting in the South is fierce. God keep you safe, Jeremy," said Henry solemnly. "News comes of terrible battles. They tell of one strange fighting team Morgan has, a grizzled old rifleman and a young Oneida Indian who stand side by side, one reloading while the other fires. I was wondering if they could possibly be that extraordinary pair you told me about. They were at Monmouth, I remember."

"Thompson and Doah-darie-yagey! It must be! They weren't—"

"Killed? No," Henry laughed, "from all I hear they're invincible."

Sam ran in with a package and a letter in his hand. He shook his head and winked at William.

William winked back. "Look's like a lady's handwriting."

Jeremiah opened the package first. Inside the paper were six New Year's cakes wrapped in a snow-white linen towel.

December 27, 1780

Dear Jeremiah,

I meant to write sooner, but we have been in a tizzy with wedding preparations. Major Hamilton and our Miss Betsy were married here in the South Parlor. It was a very happy time.

I was proud to hear you might go south to General Greene. It does seem a roundabout way to get the British out of New York so we can have our coffee house-bookstore some day, but I guess you and the General know what you're about.

The New Year's cakes may be all crumbs by the time you get them. I sent them mostly for luck anyway. Just think, a whole new year is about to begin again. All sorts of wonderful things might happen. One wonderful thing I know of for sure, is that you will come of age.

I hope you will write whenever you can, because I shall be thinking about you and, I expect, worrying a little too.

Yr friend
Nancy

P. S. Yr Horse, Rebel, is fine. She is getting old, of

course, and a little lame, but her spirit is as high as the day you left her here. We'll both be waiting, my dear Jeremiah, for you to come back.

Henry, William, and Sam had walked off a little way while Jeremiah read his letter. Henry was discussing Arnold's treason with his brother.

"Such a man's conscience must be a continuous torment to his dying day. A man, either British or American, who lets his love of gold lead him into betrayal of his country!"

Roger, too, Jeremiah thought, had such a conscience to live with until he died, or his own ruffians murdered him.

Poor Roger. He felt sorry for him. That's why, Jeremiah realized now, he hadn't minded in the least when, during their last meeting, he'd been called a sweeper boy again. The bookseller's sweeper boy! The contemptuous name no longer had the angry power to hurt him. In fact, he discovered, he was proud of it—proud of having had to work to "be somebody," first a volunteer, then an ensign, a lieutenant, and now a captain.

With a deep rush of thankfulness he realized he was more than Captain Jeremiah Cutler of the Continental Army. To the Knoxes he was still warmly regarded as a younger brother. To Sam he would always be a Son of Liberty. To Nancy Star he had become "My dear Jeremiah."

Bibliography

Brooks, Noah: Henry Knox, Soldier of Revolution. Putnam, 1899.
Crawford, Mary Caroline: Old Boston Days and Ways. Little, Brown, 1909.
Field Artillery Journal, Vol. XXIII, pages 542–549.
Flick, Alexander C: New York State Historical Association Journal IX, April, 1926, pages 119–135.
Van de Water, Frederic Franklyn: Lake Champlain and Lake George. Bobbs-Merrill, 1946.
Van Doren, Carl Clinton: Secret History of the American Revolution. Viking, 1941.
Ward, Christopher Longstreth: War of the Revolution, 2 vols. Macmillan, 1952.
Schuyler Mansion, Fort Ticonderoga Museum and New York State Museum.